THROUGH STREAMS OF TIME

For Mary + George —
God Bless and Thanks
For Your Support Through
The Years!
Chuck
2006

Other books by Charles Emery Dobbins

"Through My Angel's Eyes"
2003
Penned under the name "Emery Charles"

"The Journey Of Jeremiah Tatum"
2005

THROUGH STREAMS OF TIME

❀

Book Two Of The Kalatar Series

A Novel

Charles Emery Dobbins

iUniverse, Inc.
New York Lincoln Shanghai

Through Streams Of Time
Book Two Of The Kalatar Series

Copyright © 2006 by Charles Emery Dobbins

All rights reserved. No part of this book may be used or reproduced by any means, graphic, electronic, or mechanical, including photocopying, recording, taping or by any information storage retrieval system without the written permission of the publisher except in the case of brief quotations embodied in critical articles and reviews.

iUniverse books may be ordered through booksellers or by contacting:

iUniverse
2021 Pine Lake Road, Suite 100
Lincoln, NE 68512
www.iuniverse.com
1-800-Authors (1-800-288-4677)

This is a work of fiction. All of the characters, names, incidents, organizations and dialogue in this novel are either the products of the author's imagination or are used fictitiously.

ISBN-13: 978-0-595-41450-5 (pbk)
ISBN-13: 978-0-595-85800-2 (ebk)
ISBN-10: 0-595-41450-8 (pbk)
ISBN-10: 0-595-85800-7 (ebk)

Printed in the United States of America

For my family
God has blessed us all
Jeremiah 29:11-12

"Time is but a stream I go a-fishin in."

—Henry Thoreau

Acknowledgments

For those who are part-time writers, it's always hard to find ample time to spend on our projects. Careers tend to get in the way of our hobbies.

So it is with me.

This story was enduring in my mind, but finding time to put words onto a page is always at a premium. I could catch a few minutes at lunchtime…or a weekend get-away would find me tapping away at the computer. But real progress was always made in the late night hours. It's a time when the imagination runs wild and the speed of my typing couldn't keep up with my thoughts. It's a time when characters did more daring feats than in my daylight hours.

That is why we have copy-editors. They polish the manuscript and correct the errors that occur when the author is deprived of sleep and thinks little of grammar or punctuation. I've had the unique pleasure of working with Sarah (Stecion) Jones on this project. Not only is she quite capable in her skills, but has been a family friend for years. She helped put all the commas in the proper places and offered suggestions that enhanced the overall quality of this book. *Thank you again, Sarah.*

My thanks are also extended to some other great friends of mine. Douglas Deitle spent hours reading rough drafts and giving me his honest opinion on different points of the story. His views were always welcomed.

Ronald Davis helped with numerous versions of the graphics which will help the reader navigate through Salem Town.

A portion of this story was written while relaxing at Judith Wilke's hide-away at Lake Buckhorn, in Millersburg, Ohio. A special thanks to her for her generous hospitality. The sunroom overlooking the lake was a true inspiration.

Finally, I need to give special thanks to my wife Diane. She is always encouraging and supportive of my writing endeavors. Her love is the model used to portray the characters in my stories. It is patient and kind, never harsh or abrasive. It's a good thing to have a wife who is also your best friend.

C.E.D.

Introduction

Is there room in your life for a little fantasy?

We love adventure. Some of us grew up reading about the exploits of superheroes in comic books. Saturday afternoon matinees attracted us like moths to a flame. Early horror films, with their "state-of-the-art" special effects, kept us on the edge of our seats.

As we grew older, we turned to spy novels and James Bond movies. The action was more thrilling, and we marveled how each hero could escape impossible situations and beat the overwhelming odds to save the world.

However, somewhere along the line we grew up. We "put away childish things" and concentrated on *real* life. The cares of the world crowded in on us, and we began to worry about our daily existence.

I believe there's still room in our lives for a bit of fantasy. We can spend time addressing the "adult" concerns in our lives, yet still enjoy some things from our youth.

This book continues the story of Joshua and Corsair. They're among an elite group of mortals living in a spiritual and heavenly realm who have been chosen to fight on behalf of other humans in the spiritual arena. I trust you'll enjoy this faith-based fantasy which will take you, for a short time, to another place and time far away from the problems *we* face each day.

CHAPTER 1

The smoke was bad. Joshua could hardly breathe, let alone see where he was going. He had to be careful because flames would instantly appear from gaps in the rock formations along the way. This was a dark, unholy cavern. The subterranean passage spiraled continually downward with walkways that extended like fingers off of the main corridor. His stomach knotted as he continued forward.

He raised his flaming sword high above his head, using it as a torch to see by. It would also serve as a beacon that Corsair might notice and be drawn to. Joshua sensed she was near, but couldn't see or hear her. There were constant ungodly shrieks that assaulted his ears, making it difficult to hear his own voice. *There's no way I'll hear her in this.*

With each passing minute he became more impatient. She had to be hurt or she would have met him at their rendezvous location. He inched forward, the ground pulsing beneath his feet as if some demonic machinery was buried below in the heart of this deep, dark cavern.

And then out of nowhere, a devilish projectile came hurling towards his head. With a quick twist of the wrist, Joshua's flaming sword rendered it helpless as it disintegrated into a powder that floated to rest at his feet.

"Corsair!" His voice echoed in his head. *Where is she?* He should have been able to tell where she was. This had never happened before. In the past, they were always connected in some way while in battle. They fought as one, and each had become an extension of the other. They were two individuals who were unchanging. They were continually in touch, steadfast in battle, and constant in love. No other mortals have ever had the kind of relationship that these two had.

Joshua sensed a growing fear from deep within. This was immediately troubling because fear wasn't an emotion a Kalatar should experience. As warriors who fought on behalf of other humans in a spiritual environment, he had mastered the control of such feelings. It was the enemy who would become fearful at the sight of the flaming sword he carried and the colorful protective battle garb he wore.

The fear that began to grip him dulled his senses for a moment…and a moment was all that the enemy needed. Joshua felt the attack when he should have sensed it coming. A small devilish ghoul attacked from above, dropping onto his back. It's long, bony fingers reached around Joshua's throat and squeezed with an unholy strength.

Joshua dropped to the ground and rolled onto his back forcing the wind from the lungs of his attacker. The flame from his sword retracted leaving a short silver blade that extended from the hilt, which bore the special emblem of the Kalatar.

In one swift motion, he drove his sword behind him and into the side of the enemy. With a twist and upward thrust, the enemy released its hold and rolled away.

A mini-victory should build confidence, but for some reason Joshua became more confused and frustrated—a deadly combination. *What's going on? Where's Corsair!* His mind whirled with anxiety and doubt. His body began to shake, and his vision blurred.

An arrow struck his protective trench coat, and its color slowly changed from the combative red that the enemy feared to a grayish muted color. Joshua turned to see where the attack originated. At that instant, hordes of monsters poured out of each connecting passageway.

Due to sheer numbers, Joshua was soon engulfed and buried beneath the advancing forces. Rock-hard fists pummeled his body. Again and again, the blows rained down until Joshua began to lose consciousness.

As the smoke rose from the floor of the subterranean passage, Joshua was able to see across the cavern. There, just a few short feet away, lay

Corsair. Her motionless body lay twisted, and she showed no signs of life. It was the last thing he'd see before closing his eyes in defeat.

Then, suddenly, he heard a loud klaxon-sounding device. The noise permeated the area of battle. The smoke lifted, the enemy hordes disappeared, and all that was left were Joshua and Corsair, alone and defeated. The battle simulation had ended.

CHAPTER 2

❁

The area became a whirl of activity. Attendants rushed in and quickly whisked Corsair away. Joshua sat upright as others in The Order gathered around to tend to him. In all his years as a Kalatar, Joshua never had a training simulation go so wrong. The fear and indecision were unprecedented, yet it had been so real.

The heavenly compound where Joshua lived and trained was definitely a very special location. In all of heaven, only this area was designated for humans. They lived and worked together. They trained with one another for special operations the Creator might deem best suited for a mortal to participate in.

They also had the unique opportunity to interact with specific angels assigned to be God's liaisons between the Kalatar and the unseen hierarchy of command.

"What happened?" Joshua queried, wiping blood from his face.

"We're looking into it." The response was from Silva, a regular who'd been a Kalatar for years.

"We've never seen anything like this before," echoed another.

Joshua was weak and wobbled as he stood to his feet with the help of two others. Something was terribly wrong. "where have they taken Corsair?"

"To her quarters," Silva replied. "They'll try to treat her there. I'm sure she'll be all right."

When a Kalatar was injured in battle, the normal procedure was to get some rest and relaxation. These battle-scarred warriors needed only time to heal most wounds. A few of the heavenly healing fruits afforded them would always perk them right up. Then, usually some R&R in some exotic earthly location would help heal the wounds that required more time.

A Kalatar that died in the service of the Creator would be provided a full military funeral like none on earth, and would then be ushered into the presence of the King of Kings just like any other Christian who might pass away.

This incident, however, was different. No Kalatar had ever received more than minor injuries during training. The simulations were very real indeed, but it would serve no purpose to have a warrior injured critically, since they may be needed at a moment's notice. These training sessions were meant to hone their skills, not injure the combatants.

"I've got to get to her," Joshua moaned as he started forward. "She wasn't touched in battle, I would have sensed that. Whatever's happened to her has never happened before, I just know it."

🍁 🍁 🍁

Joshua's head cleared as he made his way to Corsair's quarters. They adjoined his personal quarters. Corsair and Joshua were more than fellow Kalatar. They shared a love for each other that was truly unique. It was unmatched anywhere in heaven or earth.

Making his way through the shiny metallic-like hallways, memories flooded his mind as he thought of how their lives had become so intertwined. It seemed like an eternity ago that they'd first met....

His thoughts were interrupted as he approached the doorway leading to Corsair's suite. The light was subdued, and all was silent. As he entered the room, he saw Corsair lying on a bed, surrounded by aides. She was dressed in white linen, and covered with white cotton-like blankets. She appeared to shiver as Joshua entered the room.

A large angelic being stood head and shoulders above everyone assembled there. As he turned, Joshua saw that it was Lucius, their unit commander.

"What's wrong with her?" Joshua asked.

"We're not sure at this point." His voice was calm and clear.

"What do you mean by that? This is heaven, for crying out loud! You have to know!" Joshua's intensity wasn't lost on the holy being he addressed.

The huge angel seemed to increase in stature as he thoughtfully addressed Joshua. "I mean we're not sure at *this* point. In all of ages past, this has never happened before. It doesn't appear to be an injury. What we do know is that Corsair appears to be dying, and we don't know why.

"Yes, this is heaven; however, this situation is extraordinary. The High Council is in session right now discussing it. No mortal has ever died while in the confines of this sanctuary. We don't take this situation lightly."

Joshua turned his attention to Corsair. Her long auburn hair lay sweaty and matted. Her dark green eyes, once the focal point of his attraction to her, remained open but void, staring into space. As Joshua drew closer, she shivered once again, as if the closer in proximity he came to her, the more pain she experienced. He stepped back.

"What can we do for her?"

Lucius gave Joshua a puzzled look, and after a long pause replied, "Why...pray, of course."

In all of Joshua's years as a Kalatar, he was the one who fought the good fight. He was the one to stand in the gap for mankind. He was the one who a mere mortal might mistake for an angel. He had powers and skills that no one on earth could dream of. He'd engaged the very powers of hell and been victorious. He had heaven as his sanctuary yet was powerless in this moment. "Of course...pray," he muttered.

❦ ❦ ❦

Hours must've passed. Joshua lost track of time. He prayed, of course. He felt his faith was being tested. This was heaven. God could do anything. It would be such a small thing for Him to heal Corsair. What purpose would be served to allow a champion to die within heaven's gates?

He alone kept the silent vigil inside Corsair's quarters. Others of The Order stood watch outside. Corsair, still unresponsive, seemed to be even more distant. Her color looked paler as time passed.

Joshua's thoughts drifted back to their first meeting. Working as a field rep for a pharmaceutical company, he'd met Corsair who had prearranged their meeting so she could introduce Joshua to his adventuresome future. They fell in love. It was a love that Corsair knew could have consequences. From their first meeting through their early victories, it seemed they were meant to be together.

Joshua looked across the room at Corsair. Her only movement came as he approached her bed. *What's wrong? Why do you seem troubled when I come closer?* He puzzled over this until he finally dozed off.

Joshua was awakened by Silva with a slight nudge to the shoulder. "It's time; the High Council has summoned us."

CHAPTER 3

The council chamber was laid out like an amphitheater. The floor of the room had a large table in the center with 12 chairs situated around it. From that point, there were 12 tiers of theater-style seats that rose upward. A standing-room gallery circled the entire room at the very top. Lighting seemed to radiate from the walls and filled the room with a soft glow.

Joshua took a seat at one end. Others of The Order filed in and filled the seats one by one. One seat remained empty. This group of 11 would be the only attendants today. The group kept silent until their unit commander, Lucius, entered the room. He circled the room slowly as if searching for the words to begin.

Joshua's mind flashed back to the first time he'd sat in this room with Corsair at his side. He'd been new to this life, and Corsair was a battle-scarred veteran. He wanted to prove himself worthy, while she only wanted him to be cautious and not feel overconfident. Overconfidence could get you killed. One warrior in their unit was in fact killed on his first mission. His thoughts returned to the present as his unit commander prepared to speak.

When Lucius spoke, his words didn't have the boldness these Kalatar were used to hearing. There was a hint of apprehension. That, in itself, was disconcerting. The Order was used to strong, decisive leadership. The being that stood before them was a High Angel, a heavenly spirit.

Lucius started the meeting as he did all others. "We seem to have a situation." Members of this unit were accustomed to a pause before he would proceed further. This time the pause seemed endless.

"The High Council has met and they've discovered the source of Corsair's 'problem.' The enemy has launched an attack that could have serious ramifications. Corsair seems to be the target of the attack. If the assault isn't stopped, and the enemy succeeds, not only will Corsair die, but in addition, all of her triumphs through the centuries will be negated. This could shake the very foundation of the world."

"How could this happen?" asked Ged, one of the 11. "There have been no attacks in this place."

"If Corsair's in danger, then we're all in danger," another added.

"If the attack is successful, any of this Order who may have joined after Corsair will cease to exist," replied Lucius. "In fact, this attack could tip the balance of power in favor of Lucifer himself!"

"That's impossible!" shouted Tobiatha. "We're all aware of what Holy Scripture has to say about Satan and his defeat! That can't be changed by anything hell's forces might try!" Others of The Order chimed in with similar comments to one another.

Lucius regained control of the meeting with an upraised hand. "What the Bible has to say about the end times is true. However, even though the enemy knows his final destiny, he never stops trying to change the ultimate outcome."

"Then where and how did this attack take place?" queried Abecca, a grizzled old veteran. "We've seen no evidence of enemy activity!"

"How this attack happened is linked with *when* it happened." Lucius continued. "We all know that God is omnipresent, and omnipotent. He is all-powerful through all of time and space. He is everywhere in every time period.

"We are not. We move through time and space in a linear plane. Even though we angels are immortal, we move through time as you do. You Kalatar, though immortal in a sense, also move through time as you did while living on earth. Your longevity is one of the benefits of being in this spiritual realm and fighting for others of your kind.

"Satan and his forces must also move through time as we do. Satan is not omnipresent as God is. He had a beginning, and his end is assured.

"However, being ever persistent, the forces of evil found a way to create a crack in the time continuum. It was quickly sealed off, but not before at least three of our Creator's enemies slipped through. This'll never happen again, but it appears that their plan is to kill Corsair before she has the opportunity to join The Order!"

The group around the table all reacted as one. They all stood and began to shout at Lucius and each other. All of them understood the ramifications an enemy victory would mean to each of them and to The Order.

Only one person didn't participate in the outburst. Joshua sat quietly, looking straight ahead, his thoughts only on Corsair. It appeared that if she died, they all died. Satan wins. That was the ominous message Lucius delivered. While the others argued and discussed the possibilities, Joshua quickly and silently left the room.

※ ※ ※

The lighting in Corsair's room was subdued. As Joshua entered, she stirred; a soft moan escaped her lips. He felt the need to touch her, to hold her. But as he again tried to reach her, she grew more agitated as if living a nightmare. She reacted as if she was experiencing physical pain. He backed off a little.

"What is it about me that troubles you so much, Corsair?" Joshua hung his head as he stepped back into the hallway. He crossed the hall, slumped down to the floor, and watched Corsair through the open doorway. Others would come and go, each one praying for Corsair and encouraging Joshua.

Time passed until Joshua was again alone with his thoughts and the motionless form of Corsair's body. Time passed as he struggled once more to maintain vigilance. Time passed until he again surrendered to the sleep his body so desperately needed.

CHAPTER 4

❀

Joshua was awakened by a slight nudge on the shoulder. Ged hovered over him with a concerned look on his face. Joshua rubbed his eyes and groaned as he rose from his seated position, his body resisting the change in position. Even here, in this heavenly compound, a mortal body was susceptible to simple aches and pains.

"It's time to rise and shine!" Ged didn't know what else to say. Joshua just grunted.

Ged was a former firefighter who had joined The Order some time after Joshua. As with other Kalatar, he had few, if any, relatives left on earth. He and Joshua had formerly lived in the same area of the country in the same time period, so they had a lot in common. They'd become fast friends.

There were many times during leisure periods when they would discuss their favorite sports teams. It was during these times they felt like the luckiest guys in the universe. Here they were—sitting in heaven, no less—discussing the Cleveland Browns or Cleveland Indians. They joked about how life couldn't get any better than that. Light humor always helped to alleviate the reality that at any instant they might be required to give their lives to save another.

Joshua gave a longing gaze into the open doorway across the hall. Nothing there had changed. He knew better than to attempt to enter.

"They're waiting for us." Ged turned to leave as he spoke. "I believe a plan of action's been decided on."

Joshua watched him start down the hall and, giving one last look at Corsair, followed him. He wasn't sure if that would be his last look at her or if the High Council's strategy would foil the enemy's plan.

❦   ❦   ❦

Once more they made their way to the council chamber. This time, the large arena was full. There was a lot of commotion among the attendees as each had their own ideas of the course of action that should be taken.

Since Corsair and Joshua were under the command of Lucius, those 12 Kalatar would normally be seated around the table waiting to be briefed on their next assignment. As it was the last time they were there, the seat next to Joshua would remain empty.

The first few tiers of seating around the room were reserved for others of The Order. No one but the highest level of command knew how many Kalatar existed at any one time. Even now there could be numerous missions in progress with the number of combatants unknown to all but their various unit commanders.

Never before had so many Kalatar been in one place at one time. Many in the chamber wore similar heavenly garb, but the one thing that set those of The Order apart was the distinctive insignia they wore signifying their rank as mortal warriors.

This unique badge, oval in shape, was worn with honor by all who'd been accepted into the ranks of Kalatar. Multi-colored jewels, like none on earth, were set against a black background. These spectacular gems looked like stars shining on a moon-lit night. In the very center was a small flaming sword pointing upward as if raised in battle by an unseen hand.

All who were entrusted with this emblem also carried a life-size duplicate of the sword attached to their belts. Its craftsmanship was unmatched. The hilt was beautifully engraved and also bore the insignia of the Kalatar. The handle was of pure ivory, yet seemed to miraculously mold itself to fit the hand of its owner. This was a powerful weapon that would instantly become a fiery blade when engaging an enemy.

Some of those redeemed by the blood of the Lamb occupied the next few tiers: mortals, who had lived their lives on earth, accepted the salvation offered by Christ's sacrifice, and had died. Their spirits now awaited the resurrection of their mortal bodies, which would take place when the final trumpet sounded signaling the start of end-time events.

Those spirit beings looked like a who's who of biblical saints and scholars. The 12 disciples who followed Jesus and some of the great writers of Scripture attended. Paul, Timothy, Barnabas, and other New Testament missionaries were there as well.

Higher up in the gallery were tiers that would be occupied by different classes of heavenly beings. Angels, cherubim, and seraphim, along with other heavenly spirits never mentioned in the Holy Scriptures, filled available positions.

There was a special section, front and center, with two places reserved for two remarkable individuals. In an unprecedented move, two mortals who'd never made an appearance here before settled in to watch the proceedings. Those already in their seats watched in awe as this pair entered and moved to their seats.

Enoch and Elijah, dressed in white flowing garments, sat stoically, waiting for the meeting to start. Elijah had long white hair and a neatly trimmed beard. Enoch was quite bald, but also displayed a beard; his, however, was much longer than Elijah's. They talked with each other and occasionally pointed to certain things around the large room.

It was becoming apparent that the outcome of this situation would directly impact *their* future. Not only theirs, but all of mankind. History and all future events could be changed forever. The Creator, after all, had a plan for them in His intended future. It was a roll they would play out in end-time events.

The murmuring in the amphitheater grew silent as 12 heavenly beings entered the room. Lucius was one of the 12. They circled the room once and positioned themselves at equal intervals around the perimeter. They were impressive not only in stature, but also because these 12 were unit commanders…and being all together in one place gave everyone in attendance a positive count of the number of Kalatar that existed.

There was no sound from the gallery now. All eyes were on the doorway. Everyone could only speculate as to who would enter the room next. The hierarchy of command above the level of unit commander had always been a mystery. Everyone knew there was a High Council, but nothing more. It was never something they needed to concern themselves with. The decisions were always proper and right.

Lucius stepped forward and quietly advised his unit to leave the table and join the others of The Order in the gallery. It was becoming evident that the place of honor at the conference table would be reserved for the High Council. The 11 filtered upward and settled in among their comrades.

They had just settled into their seats when a soft murmur began to spread through the crowded room. As the first shadow entered the doorway, those in the conference center rose to their feet to honor the High Council. Everyone was shocked and in awe as they saw who the members of this council were.

CHAPTER 5

As the 12 members of the High Council entered the room, for some curious reason, they were recognizable to all assembled. They wore long flowing robes and appeared to float effortlessly across the room. These were spirit beings, but not just any spirit beings.

These were 12 earthly champions who'd lived and died and were now serving the Creator in this capacity: leaders of the greatest fighting team of mortals ever assembled. They each found a seat around the table, and 11 sat down—while one remained standing.

Joshua and the others of The Order were pleased to see that the members of this council were some of the greatest warriors of biblical times. As they looked around the table, the exploits of these 12 were renewed in their minds once more.

Moses was the leader of Israel as they fled from Pharaoh's army, escaping through the parted waters of the Red Sea. Later he led Israel into battle against the Amalekites. Israel persevered as long as Moses held his staff high above his head signifying God's presence with the troops.

Joshua was one of the original 12 spies sent to investigate the area God had promised Israel. As Israel moved into the land, Joshua destroyed the heathen nations as God instructed.

Deborah was a prophetess of God, and lead Israel during the time they were governed by judges. She followed Barak into battle against Sisera of Canaan to offer advice as the Lord directed.

Barak was the leader in that conflict and lead 10,000 men in a complete route of Sisera and his forces.

Jephthah the Gileadite was a mighty warrior. He was called upon by his leaders to become the commander of their forces. He engaged the armies of Ammon and devastated twenty towns before the victory was complete.

Gideon was an Israelite called to arms by an angel of the Lord. He would have the privilege of hearing that angel declare to him, "The Lord is with you, mighty warrior." With that, Gideon defeated the vast army of the Midianites with only 300 men.

Samson as a young man killed a lion with his bare hands. Later in his life, he killed 1,000 men with the jawbone of a donkey. At the end of his life, he brought the pillars of a large amphitheater down…and in his death, he destroyed more of Israel's enemies than he did during his lifetime.

David, King of Israel, fought and killed the Philistine champion Goliath as a young boy. Later, his military exploits would cause women to sing, "Saul has killed his thousands, but David has killed his ten thousands!"

Jonathan was David's best friend. As a warrior, he, along with his armor bearer, killed 20 Philistines. The battle took place in a half-acre field, and the fighting was so fierce that it caused the entire enemy army to flee.

Asa was a king of Judah. As he prayed, God directed him to go and engage the army of the Cushites. That day, he defeated a vast army totaling tens of thousands.

Jephoshaphat was a king of Judah as well. He defeated the immense armies of Moab and Ammon. The victory was so complete that it took three days to carry away the plunder.

Esther was a Jewish girl in exile with her fellow countrymen in Persia. As she found favor with King Xerxes, she rose to become queen of the land. Through her leadership, the entire Jewish population was saved from extinction as the evil Haman sought to destroy them all.

Those reflecting on these great accomplishments had their attention drawn back to the present as David rose from his seat to speak. He was tall and handsome and appeared younger in spirit than he was at the time of his death. David died at the age of 70, having reigned a total of 40 years. A hush fell over the vast assembly as this great king started to address the gathering.

"Fellow members of the High Council, members of The Order of Kalatar, honorable heavenly hosts, and all heavenly creatures great and small in attendance, I welcome you to this unprecedented caucus to discuss the grave matters before us.

"I also welcome our two distinguished guests, Enoch and Elijah, who we all know have an acute interest in our proceedings this hour. Our decisions here will greatly impact their ultimate mission as set before them by our Lord, the Great God Jehovah.

"My fellow celestial citizens, our arch enemy Lucifer is ever hard at work in trying to change the outcome of his final destiny and has struck a blow that could shake the very core of our existence. No one on this illustrious council could ever have imagined as bold a move as he's taken. In fact, we would not have thought such a move was even possible.

"The military minds around this table all agree that the strategy taken by the enemy is as cunning as it is bold, and the probability of success is quite high. This unprecedented move has caused a great deal of debate in our chambers, and different plans of counter-attack have been discussed at great lengths."

King David took a moment here, as if to collect his thoughts. He slowly made his way around the chamber so he could address more sections in a more direct manner. Since he didn't possess a mortal, physical body, he did in fact move about the room floating a few inches above the floor.

He looked up into the crowd and continued: "My friends, the rumors you may have heard are true. Satan's forces have made their way back in time to launch this attack. The focus of their attack is a highly respected member of The Order of Kalatar. Her name is Corsair. They've chosen the era some would call the late 17th century. The location is North America, in an area known as Massachusetts. It's in a time period that precedes Corsair's invitation to join the ranks of these courageous mortals who sit with us this day. It's a time in which she is quite vulnerable, and in grave danger."

There was a quiet murmur that could be heard around the room, and a reverent air of anticipation gripped all. Tension was high. "This council is comprised of a diverse group of leaders, and their particular styles all lead toward good discussions. Various plans have been discussed. Some influential members favored an all-out assault on the enemy, bringing all the powers at heaven's command to bear on these spiritual terrorists. For some pointed reasons, this can not be our plan of attack.

"Two members of our team, after numerous heated discussions, have come up with a plan that will allow us the best chance of success. I'll now relinquish the floor to one of these two, who have so eloquently made their case in such a crisis situation as this. Joshua, the floor is yours."

❦   ❦   ❦

At the mention of this Old Testament leader, some members of The Order in the gallery turned and smiled at Joshua. He'd taken the name of Joshua when he joined their ranks. It wasn't unusual for new recruits to change their names for various reasons. Joshua felt that his original earthly name was inappropriate for use as a Kalatar, so he picked the name of Joshua to use. He felt it was a name with strong character and would make a statement that he was serious about emulating the fighting character of his namesake.

The older, gray-haired Joshua moved slowly from his seat to address the assembly. Being a spirit being, age or mortal feebleness had no effect on him. It appeared to be a characteristic of his to move in a deliberate manner. As he began to speak, one could tell he also chose his words carefully.

"Thank you. I'm sure…that those assembled here care not to be bored…with the inner workings of this council. Suffice it to be said that our discussions…and the conclusions drawn of this matter…have been weighed heavily on our hearts…and our minds."

The pauses were distracting to some of those listening, but all felt the intensity and the passion evoked as Joshua continued. "After much consideration, a plan for an all-out assault…was abandoned. We felt that it might do more harm…than good. My experiences brought to light the belief…that a clandestine operation…would be best.

"As I was one of the original 12 spies…sent into the land of Canaan, I know first-hand…that the information from that action changed the course of human events…for the following 40 years.

"In this case, the enemy…will be expecting an all-out assault, and we believe that their operatives…are already fully entrenched…into the culture of that day. They may elicit some minor help from the spiritual realm of that era, but…we believe they may be…as foreign to the evil forces of that time…as they will be to the forces of good.

"Since this operation will be covert in nature, a small force, working undercover…to discover the enemy's plan, is advised. One other member of our council…is yet to speak, and you'll learn of our final plan, and how it is to be carried out. I now relinquish the floor to Queen Esther."

CHAPTER 6

A soft murmur swept the crowded room as some speculated what input Queen Esther could possibly have. Esther, above all others, seemed out of place on the council. Here among a band of grizzled old war veterans was a beautiful young spirit. Certainly she was a rose among a group of thorns.

Esther had never led a revolt. She hadn't marched into battle as Deborah had. Some questioned her qualifications. Her beauty had helped her rise to power in ancient Persia. In fact, much of what she'd accomplished came as a result of advice from her cousin Mordecai. King Xerxes was so smitten with her beauty that he was willing to please her in any way he could. God had certainly worked through her situation there to save an entire race.

As Esther rose to address the congregation, those mortal men in attendance quickly admitted (at least in thought) that Esther was without a doubt an extraordinary beauty. Holy Scriptures had described her as "lovely in form and features." All eyes followed her every movement. All ears were tuned for her first words. It was quite hypnotic. This moment wasn't lost on her. She smiled impishly as she took over Joshua's place on the conference floor.

"My, my, my...look what's brought us all here today, my friends. What a great and awesome God we serve!" Her somewhat cheerful manner of speaking and her fluid body language seemed to relieve the tension in the room. Her voice had a melodious quality about it that had a calming effect on all those who were listening. One could almost picture Esther standing before King Xerxes presenting her case to him that would ultimately save the Jewish nation. He would have been as mesmerized by her as those in attendance were this day.

"We all stand here today as a testimony to the great and magnificent power of the Great God Jehovah! What a privilege we've had to serve Him! Would you all not agree?"

There was a ripple of excitement throughout the crowd as she spoke. What had been a comfortless assemblage just minutes before was now beginning to perk up a bit as heads nodded in agreement to the words spoken by the former queen.

"Come now, my friends…agree with me!"

Now the congregation joined in as all around the conference hall words came ringing back at her.

"Yes!"

"Absolutely!"

"Without a doubt!"

"Amen!"

Now heads turned toward one another, and a few smiles could be seen as the mood lifted around the room.

Esther continued, now with a wide smile, "Yes, a privilege indeed! We're all witnesses of God's great power! Every mortal here has had the experience of Jehovah's great power working through him or her! God…is…good!

"Today, we are assembled at the very footstool of the ultimate power of the universe! Now I ask you, my friends, what have we to fear? Lucifer's power may be great. Lucifer's plan may be great. Lucifer's legions may be great. But," and with that word hanging on the tip of her tongue, Esther looked around. Every ear knew what was coming next. "But…Jehovah is greater!"

Several shouts of "Amen!" came ringing from every corner of the large conference center. Winged creatures left their perches and flew back and forth singing praises to God. Folks stood and cheered. Esther's approach had the needed effect. The mood had definitely changed.

Esther stood and waited for the congregation to settle back into their seats. She had accomplished her first goal. She wasn't acting as a celestial cheerleader, but simply reminding those present of God's faithfulness, and setting the stage for her next remarks.

"My friends...from the dawn of time God has chosen man to have a part in working His perfect will. Abraham was one man, chosen by Jehovah to be the father of many nations. Rahab was one woman who helped the spies at Jericho. Jehosheba, a nurse, hid the baby Joash for six years to keep him from being murdered by Queen Athaliah. John the Baptist was one voice crying in the wilderness to prepare for the coming of the Messiah."

Esther paused here to look around, letting her point sink in. She brought her hands together before her as if in prayer as she continued. "The Son of God chose to become one man to save all mankind.

"The plan we've chosen has precedence. Although the action to be taken will be covert in nature, we've decided that one man will undertake it. It will be a member of The Order of Kalatar, Joshua by name."

It started as a low murmur, but quickly grew in volume as those around the room questioned this decision. As the decision sunk in, voices could be heard. "No! Send me!" one would shout. "More, more warriors are needed!" came from another area. "Angels, we need angelic beings for this!" from the upper tiers.

The 11 seated around the table rose to their feet as Esther raised her hands for silence. The 12 moved closer together as she spoke. This time the words had the authority of a ruler.

"This council will NOT be questioned or second-guessed! The decisions we make are final! However, because of the gravity of this situation, I'll make an exception this once, to explain why we've chosen this course of action.

"Kalatar Joshua has been chosen because of his close relationship with Corsair. Before he joined their ranks, he had a connection, a link, with Corsair. We believe that as he interacts with her in the distant past, there'll be something that will draw her to him. Their love for each other, we're hoping, will be a point of contact."

As Joshua sat in stunned silence, he considered the possibility of traveling into the past to meet and rescue Corsair. He vividly remembered his first meeting with her, and how he was drawn to her. It was as if they were meant to be together from the beginning.

A slight rumble, that swept through the heavenly chambers they were meeting in, interrupted his thoughts. All those in attendance froze. No one could imagine what had happened. Mortals in attendance thought it was an earthquake, although that couldn't possibly be the case.

Esther gathered herself and continued. "That rumbling is the first fruits of the enemy's efforts. The task before us is becoming urgent. We'll need to proceed with great haste.

"Getting back to our plan, we feel the enemy won't be expecting just one person. That person should be able to move freely without fear of exposure. One person was also chosen because of the danger of traveling into the past. Joshua may not survive, although everything will hinge on his success. Once again, Jehovah has chosen one man, and that man may sacrifice for all concerned."

With that, Esther sat down.

CHAPTER 7

❀

Time. It's a concept that is profoundly resistant to simple definition. We drift along in it. The past is just a wisp of a memory. Sometimes we struggle to remember the simplest things. We grasp at the future. We plan. We have goals that we work toward.

But in reality, we are wrapped in the present. We wear it like a cloak. We labor at times to shrug it off with no success. The future is always just out of reach, and the past is as distant as our last breath. The present is where we live. Each second is *now*, with the previous one gone forever. Or is it?

Time is an ever-running stream in which we float along with no ability to stop it, nor change it. But what if you could step out of the stream onto dry land...and walk upstream and back into time? What if you could travel back into time to save a loved one? That's the situation Joshua now found himself in.

🍁   🍁   🍁

Joshua had left the meeting room. The message and the decision were clear. He'd been chosen to travel to the distant past and prevent the enemy from killing Corsair and destroying the future, as he knew it.

He made his way through the winding corridors to Corsair's quarters. He stepped through the doorway and was shocked at what he saw.

Corsair was attended to by a number of assistants. There wasn't much they could do for her. Joshua was dismayed to see that she looked even worse than before.

Her cheeks were sunken in and hollow. Her skin was even grayer in color. Her breath came in short halting intervals, and each lungful of air seemed painful. Her body would shiver, even though she was covered from head to foot with warming blankets.

The long auburn hair that had been one of the things Joshua found most attractive about her was pulled back and tied as sweat beaded up on her forehead. Her eyes seemed to be slowly closing as if her fight was nearing the end.

Joshua inched forward, expecting an adverse reaction from the love of his life. Nothing happened. He tried another six inches, then six more. Each foot seemed to take an eternity, but with each new step he was able to move a little closer.

The attendants saw this and moved away from the bed. If Joshua was to reach Corsair, they felt they would need time alone.

Minutes passed. They seemed like hours, yet Joshua continued to inch forward, step by step. Ten feet to go, then nine, then eight…Joshua prayed as he moved forward. Now he could feel perspiration from the tension in the dimly lit room.

Three feet left to go. Joshua stopped. "Corsair," he whispered. He was almost afraid to breathe her name for fear she couldn't bear the pain that he'd seen before.

Two feet more and he'd be there. She stirred a bit, then nothing more. The veins in her neck were protruded, and battle scars from past conflicts could be seen above the gown she wore.

One foot left. So close, yet so far. Dare he reach out to her? Joshua extended a hand toward hers. *Just a touch Lord, please, just a touch.* His eyes were on her now bony hand.

As he stretched to make contact, it happened. Corsair let loose with a blood-curdling scream and she sat straight up in her bed. Joshua jumped back for an instant then closed the expanse between Corsair and himself. He took her into his arms as she opened her eyes and for an instant focused on him. "Save me, Joshua, save me!" With that, she collapsed back onto the bed and fell into a deep coma.

CHAPTER 8

Now, time *was* of the essence. Joshua couldn't bear it anymore. Time was running out for Corsair. He rushed from her room and entered his quarters. He quickly gathered the things he needed and headed out again. As if on cue, he could sense that Lucius was expecting him.

His unit met him on the way, and they proceeded to a smaller ready room. It was from there that they embarked on missions after final briefings. They could all feel the tension in the room as they entered. Lucius was there along with Esther and Joshua. The fact that two members of the High Council were present added to the stress levels of all. These two sat silently as Lucius conducted the briefing. He directed his comments to his unit and Joshua in particular.

"We'll start with a few words that'll be of great value in relieving the pressure we all feel right now. The feeling of urgency you sense is real, but unfounded. We know that Corsair is at the point of death, here and now. However, we'll be able to place Joshua far enough back in her mortal timeline that he'll be able to assess the situation long before things become critical.

"The percentage of success in transporting him to that era is the crucial part of our equation. We've never opened the time continuum at all, let alone allow a mortal to attempt to enter. Joshua may be killed at once or injured to the point he may not be able to complete his mission.

"The best estimate he'll survive the trip is 60 percent. One advantage he'll have is that he'll be traveling into the past in the spiritual realm.

From there, he will move about until he can enter the mortal regions we've targeted."

At this, Ged raised a hand to be recognized. "Will he be able to interact with Kalatar of that era, and will the enemy be aware of his presence?"

"Good points, Ged. The members of your Order won't be aware of the situation at first. As *we* discovered the enemy slipped through the time continuum into the past, they'll be aware that something's happening. They'll no doubt investigate, but it'll be a strange phenomenon. I'd like to point out that the number of Kalatar in that time period are few, and there may be little or no help available at all.

"The times since then have grown more evil, and we have added to your ranks as needed. The enemy of that time would never have encountered one as powerful as Joshua. Your powers today have evolved considerably since early times. The forces of darkness that have journeyed to kill Corsair will know Joshua when they meet him."

The thought of their abilities being greater than members of The Order in the past seemed to intrigue those around the table. Joshua and his comrades enjoyed powers the normal person could only dream of or read about in magazines. These powers would include greater physical strength and endurance, superior speed, and mental toughness. They could cloak their physical appearances to blend in with other mortals as needed. Add to these attributes special protective garments as well as their flaming swords, and these mortal warriors were definitely formidable foes.

"If there are no further questions…." and with that, Joshua raised his hand.

"Where *exactly* will I be going?"

"Correct, you're right," added Lucius. "The specific time period is around the year 1692. The location is in the state of Massachusetts, in North America. The town is called Salem, or nearby Salem Village. Since we know *our* history of Corsair, she may be working near the docks of the village. That may have already changed. We're not sure."

Abecca interjected. "Wasn't that a period of great unrest with considerable enemy activity?"

"That's true. The enemy gained quite a foothold in that era, and I'm sure that's why that period and Corsair in particular were chosen. Now…it's time. Joshua needs to be underway. Everything is prepared and ready."

🍁 🍁 🍁

The method of travel for the likes of Joshua was quite unique. When entering or leaving their heavenly compound, a Kalatar would simply concentrate on his destination and a watery wall of shimmering light would open and he would walk through as a person might walk under a waterfall. The colors were always magnificent, and the sound was deafening. The roar was like nothing on earth.

After walking through, one would exit into either the spiritual or mortal realm of whatever geographic location was intended. In the spiritual realm, he could move about as an angel would. To materialize into a physical area, he would again concentrate on his destination and, after checking to see if all was clear, would pop into a physical state. Whether in the physical or spiritual, great care had to be taken. Death could occur at any time and in any place.

Even though he'd traveled between heaven and earth many times, it still remained an awesome sight every time Joshua was confronted with the deafening roar and brilliant colors of his private gateway. It always reminded him of his special calling: to defend other mortals.

🍁 🍁 🍁

Joshua stepped from the ready room out onto a balcony for what might be his last look at his heavenly abode. He had no idea if he would ever see this spectacular view again. Winged creatures flew back and forth, over and under their floating fortress. Suspended cities, like islands in the sky, hovered at many different levels. Endless praises continued to permeate the entire atmosphere. Colors never humanly imagined had become common to these mortals, some of whom now joined Joshua on this heavenly perch.

Ged, Abecca, and Tobiatha gathered around Joshua. No one spoke for some time. They were all aware that the next few minutes could be the last for their comrade. Although they had all fought many battles against great odds, and come through victorious, death was ever present. Any one of them would gladly change places with Joshua though. To die serving the Creator was the least they could do. There could be no greater honor.

Tobiatha broke the silence. "The choice made was the best. It had to be you."

"I know." Joshua stared straight ahead.

"Our prayers are with you," said Abecca.

Joshua turned and grinned. "Of course they are. I expect no less! And when I return, what glorious stories of victories I'll have to tell!" Buoyed by his friends' presence he added, "And Corsair's to be my first vision when I return."

These gladiators took time for prayer, and with a slap on the back and a few manly hugs, this small group moved back indoors for final preparations.

CHAPTER 9

Joshua donned his protective clothing, which included lightweight but nearly indestructible shirt and pants, along with calf-high boots to protect him even in the vilest of demon-infested swamps in the spirit world.

Add to that a long trench coat possessing defensive qualities, and Joshua was an imposing force. His sharp metal-bladed sword snapped securely into its sheath on his belt. Although short in length, the blade could instantly be transformed into a flaming sword about three feet long with just a mere thought from its owner.

A few battle rations were added to hidden pockets of his coat, and Joshua was ready to be on his way. With one last look at his friends, he left the preparation area and walked back into the ready room. His comrades followed close behind.

When they entered the ready room once more, an amazing sight awaited them. Others of The Order had joined ranks along the walkway forming a gauntlet Joshua would walk through. It wasn't just an honor...but also a very real possibility that this could be his last mission. Heaven and earth hung in the balance, and they all knew it.

With a nod to Lucius, Joshua indicated his readiness. As if on cue, the opposite wall began to shimmer and melt away. Joshua and the others weren't ready for the sight before them. Instead of the colorful waterfall-like downpour they were used to, a frightful cascade of fiery lava presented itself to the heavenly warrior.

The heat, whether real or imagined, seemed unbearable. Any normal person would shrink back instead of proceeding forward. Without hesitation, Joshua charged forward and plunged into the molten mass of fire with these words resounding in his mind. "Save me, Joshua, save me!"

🍁   🍁   🍁

At first, all was black and silent. So silent that Joshua experienced ringing in his ears. The absence of light was suffocating. Limbo, nothingness, no sense of movement...or time.

Then, a sensation; it was slow at first, and then it picked up speed. It seemed to be a circular pattern, but Joshua couldn't be sure. He had nothing to fix his gaze upon so the sensation could have been real or imagined.

A small light appeared for an instant, and then it was gone. Then there was another flash...and another. *Lightning*. As he used the intermittent pulsating light as a reference, he could see now that he was moving in a circular pattern toward the lights. They increased in size the closer he moved toward them.

Something was vaguely familiar about the ever-enlarging black hole he seemed to be hurling toward. It reminded him of a bathtub drain. As water flows down a drain in a circular pattern, so he seemed to be swept along into this ominous, electrically-charged celestial gateway.

Now Joshua found himself near the point of passing out. He struggled to remain focused. The lightning flashed faster and faster as his spinning body matched the speed of the strobe lights assaulting his senses. Even with eyes closed he could *feel* the intensity increase as he neared the black portal.

Lightning, but no thunder. Strange. Not the phenomenon, but the fact that it crossed his mind. *No sound at all.* However, the closer he came to arriving at this supernatural target, the more the lightning became a constant. The light from the opening was so bright it permeated his very being. His hair rose from the electrical charge, and Joshua now wondered if this was the part of his journey that the High Council worried about. Would he survive the next few seconds?

It happened quickly, in a split second. What was total darkness, except for the once-faint light, now became a cosmic storm of light and energy. As Joshua passed through this uncharted gateway, it felt as if the energy from the electrical charges assimilated his body into this new environment. He felt stretched and pulled in every direction, then calm and at peace. He felt different, but the same.

It was at this point that the images began to appear. As if on a giant picture screen (yet in his mind, he supposed), Joshua saw his image as he jumped through the streams of lava. Then Corsair's stricken image, lying injured with attendants surrounding her bed. Next came the meeting with the High Council.

He could feel the intensity of each scene as if he were there in person. Every new image was more personal. There was Corsair, fighting by his side. And Linda Carson, the teenage girl they had rescued on his first mission as a Kalatar.

He relived again his passage into the heavenly realm for the first time and Corsair explaining to him the Creator's plan for him to help mankind in this very unique way.

Then before him was the scene where he saw Corsair for the first time. His male instincts and disgraceful thoughts at that time saw only her outward beauty, and his mind whirled with ways to meet (and bed) her. He would soon find out that there was, in reality, a higher design for him.

The pace of the images picked up, yet Joshua digested them all, one by one. Historical events he'd lived through, the fall of Communism, landing a man on the moon, the Vietnam War. He chuckled to see the newspaper headline announcing the Cleveland Browns had won the NFL championship in the year 1964. The headline of the murder of a childhood classmate, Marian Brubaker, quickly flashed before him. No one was ever brought to justice for her death.

His school days, his parents, his birth. *How odd.* Here he was able to witness his own birth and the interaction of his parents at this new gift from God. All these images were comprehensive in scope and length. Years passed by, yet all events clicked by instantaneously for Joshua.

Mental snapshots now came rapid-fire, yet were complete and unabridged. Some dealt with national issues, some had worldwide implications. Famines and floods, hurricanes and tornadoes, showing nature's fury. The Nazi's destruction of Jews and the atomic bombs dropped on Japan to end World War II indicated man could be just as destructive as nature.

Although these events caused countless deaths and sufferings, Joshua also saw events of great celebration. Of course, the end of World War II was celebrated worldwide. Events smaller in scope still riveted the world. Charles Lindbergh landed outside of Paris after the first solo flight across the Atlantic Ocean. More celebrations as World War I ended.

Then he saw great inventions that changed the course of history flash by. Man took to the air and lighted the night. Communications crossed wires strung through cities instead of messengers delivering words written on paper. Steam-driven locomotives sped across ribbons of steel as man flexed his industrial muscle.

Then…the sound of a single gunshot and a bearded man slumps forward in Ford's Theatre. A president is assassinated. Images followed that of yet another war. This one pits brother against brother, and father against son. A nation struggles with ideologies and convictions. Slavery is but one issue that catapults a nation to change…and to war with itself.

From a civil war to America's founding fathers, the scenes continued to change. Politicians and statesmen met and hammered out a constitution to guide a new country that Joshua knew would struggle to survive. He had just witnessed scenes of the brutal blood-bath that resulted from differing views of how men should govern themselves.

More war…this time a nation revolts against a king. Men band together to battle armies that crossed an ocean to enforce unjust laws of a monarch. They declare their independence on paper and in deed; and all that sign the unprecedented document paid with their fortunes and their lives, yet a nation is born.

In some small recess of Joshua's mind he realized that war and struggles are a constant part of growth. As nations contended with each other, men on both sides of the conflicts believed in their causes. As men would see things, there was always an *evil* to be overcome.

In the supernatural, Joshua continued that basic endeavor of man—to conquer evil. In this kaleidoscope of history he was privy to, he realized even more how hard Satan worked to destroy the lives and capture the souls of mankind.

Things slowed a bit, or so it seemed, for Joshua now. The centuries of time slowed to mere decades passing by. The scope of history narrowed to a portion of land near the East Coast of the Americas, 13 colonies still ruled by King George II.

As things slowed even more, Joshua could now focus more in a natural way. What had been rapid-fire scenes of history now became less of a whirl to his natural senses. His eyes seemed to open, and his gaze fixed on his surroundings and on the scenes passing by in reverse order. He could see the events of time were passing him by as he remained in a fixed position.

Trees, grass, and lush vegetation were all around him. Yet, it was like nothing he had seen in heaven or earth. Colors were ever changing and the plants seemed to wither and die if he moved a little to the left. If he changed direction and moved to the right, there seemed to be growth and life. To every thing, even here, there is a season. *"A time to live and a time to die."*

Joshua's journey was near an end. He could sense it was time for him to re-enter this ever-moving time stream. The events of time had rushed by as he'd stood on the riverbank, watching...observing.

Without hesitation, he dove headfirst into the rushing "waters." Once more the electrical storm erupted. This time, however, Joshua was spit from the mouth of the black hole and into the spiritual realm of the 17th century.

As he floated in the state he was more familiar with, Joshua looked back and saw the wall of lava, retreating into the distance. He'd survived. But could he now save Corsair...and their future?

CHAPTER 10

❈

Salem, Massachusetts was established in 1623 primarily as a fishing community. After three years of struggle on rocky, stormy Cape Ann, a group of the settlers set out to establish a more permanent settlement. They found sheltered, fertile land at the mouth of the Naumkeag River.

The new settlement, called Naumkeag, or "comfort haven," by the Native Americans, thrived on farming and fishing. In 1629, the settlement was renamed Salem for Shalom, the Hebrew word for "peace." Joshua would find it anything but peaceful.

The Puritans that arrived in Salem harbor on the ship Arbella had signed a document called the"Arbella Covenant." This document formed the basis for a theocracy in Massachusetts. This form of government concluded that the Church and the State would be one entity. There would be no difference between religion and government. The same laws would govern the Church and the State.

Salem would, in the future, become a major shipbuilding and maritime trade center. Lucrative trading routes with Asia would help this city to prosper to the point that by 1790, it would become the sixth largest city in the country. But, this was 1692, a century before that great prosperity.

This was a time when the cultures of the farming community and commercial industries of Salem would clash. The puritanical religious customs of the day were already on a collision course with history.

Even though daily life in Salem was controlled by religious values, outside influences began to make inroads into the culture. Salem essentially had become two communities. Salem Village was actually part of Salem Town, but was set apart by its economy, class, and character. Residents of Salem Village were mostly poor farmers. Salem Town was a more prosperous port town. It became the center of trade with London. Most who lived there became wealthy merchants.

Folks who lived in Salem Village tried for years to gain some form of independence from Salem Town with little success. The town depended on the farmers for food, but they were the ones who determined crop prices and collected taxes from the village. Salem Village didn't even have its own church and minister until 1674.

Add to this the fact that there was a division in Salem Village itself. Some who lived closest to Salem Town near Ipswich Road became business owners, such as blacksmiths, carpenters, and inn-keepers. These folks prospered somewhat more than their fellow villagers. Most farmers believed that the worldliness of Salem Town was creeping towards them and threatened their Puritan values. They pointed out that whaling ships and trading vessels brought sailors who didn't share the puritanical ideals of the religious leaders of the day.

As the shipping and fishing industries grew, the need for more commercial businesses grew as well. General stores sprung up. Inns provided food and shelter for sailors in between voyages. Although a modest menu was provided, sailors always seemed to find a way to find stronger drink to quench their thirst. Things were changing.

Some people in Salem Town now began to look down on their neighbors in Salem Village. They were becoming more affluent (a good thing, they thought), while villagers believed that those in the town were growing apart from the religious values their community was founded upon when the Arbella Covenant was signed.

The community as a whole was tight-knit—most folks knew just about everybody—and that's what made the events of early 1692 hard to understand. History would record this as the period of the Salem Witch Trials.

Joshua would experience first-hand the forces of evil and their influences on men and women of this time period. Innocent people would be accused of witchcraft and making pacts with the devil. Many of them would die as a result.

🍁 🍁 🍁

To digest the events of the Salem Witch Trials, it's necessary to explore the times in which accusations of witchcraft occurred.

First of all, there were the ordinary stresses of 17th century life in the Massachusetts Bay Colony. Life was hard.

There was a strong belief in the devil, factions among Salem Village families, and rivalry with nearby Salem Town. There was also the ever-present fear of a recent small pox epidemic. Attack by warring Indian tribes was a threat as well.

All these things combined to create a fertile ground for fear and suspicion.

On January 20, 1692, nine-year-old Elizabeth Parris and 11-year-old Abigail Williams, both from Salem Village, began to exhibit strange behavior. There was screaming and convulsive seizures. They would appear to be in a trance-like state at times. Soon, other young girls would follow suit in similar behavior.

By mid-February, doctors, unable to diagnose the cause of their problems, concluded that Satan was influencing the girls. Reverend Samuel Parris (no relation to Elizabeth) called for community prayers and fasting. He hoped that they would be able to drive the evil spirits away.

The girls were under great pressure to identify the source of their affliction, and they finally named three women as the witches who vexed their spirits. The three were Tituba, a Carib Indian slave, Sarah Good, and Sarah Osborne. On February 29, warrants were issued for their arrest.

Sarah Good and Sarah Osborne maintained their innocence and were imprisoned. Tituba, however, confessed to seeing the devil at times. She also indicated a conspiracy of witches at work in the community. If an accused person would admit to the charges against her and repent of her evil deeds, she was free to go. Tituba was free.

And with that, the insanity began. The list grew with each passing week. Martha Corey, Rebecca Nurse, and Elizabeth Proctor were all accused of witchcraft. Men like Nehemiah Abbott and William Hobbs fought the charges. Before all was said and done, 150 people would be charged, and 19 would be hanged.

Some would be charged merely because of their social status. There were a few women who were accused simply because they owned businesses or land. Female ownership upset the Puritan social order. That alone would make them targets. Many fine church-going women, formerly of high standing in the community, were vulnerable.

The madness continued through April and into May. On May 10, Sarah Osborne died in prison. On May 27, a new governor, Sir William Phips, appointed a special court to start the trials for those accused of witchcraft.

On June 10, Bridget Bishop became the first person to be found guilty and hanged in Salem. Before her death she stated, "I am no witch. I am innocent. I know nothing of it."

🍁 🍁 🍁

1692 Salem, Massachusetts

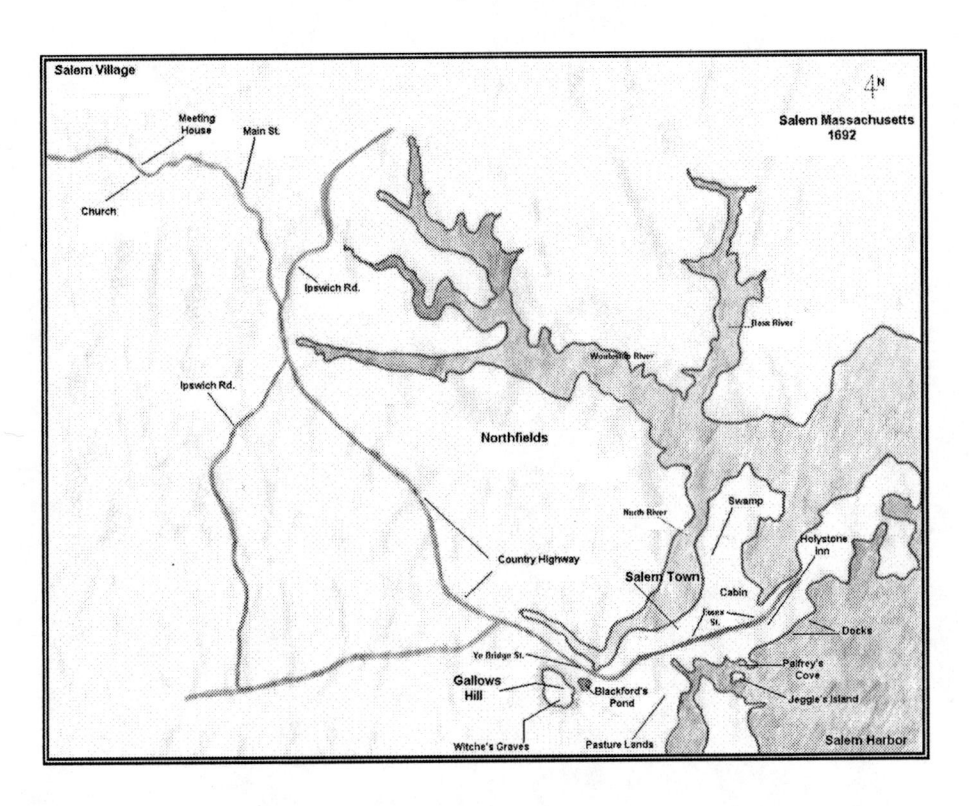

🍁 🍁 🍁

CHAPTER 11

❈

It was a cool morning in early March 1692 when Joshua popped into the mortal realm. The fog protected him from detection, but in reality, there was no one around to accidentally see him appear. This time period wasn't like the 21st century he was used to. Normally, he would have to be extremely careful about his comings and goings.

The grass was wet with dew and all was silent as Joshua stood still as a statue taking in all that his senses could focus on. There was no sound except that of a far-away bird greeting the new day. *A robin.* Joshua had never been good about identifying birds, but given the time of year, it was a good guess on his part that the robins would be returning early from their southern wintertime homes. *It should be about early March.*

He stepped into the middle of a road—a fork in a road to be exact. An old weathered road sign indicated one of the roads was named Ipswich Road. This road was the demarcation point between Salem Village and Salem Town. It ran north and south. Off to the west was Main Street, leading into Salem Village, and Country Highway to the east lead to Salem Town.

As he took in his new surroundings, Joshua tried to focus on every little thing. The wet grass was already ankle high. Wild flowers that would line the dirt road he stood on hadn't even begun to bloom yet. He imagined it would be a pretty site later in the spring and early summer.

The sun was beginning to rise in the east, and it gave him a starting point for his short journey into Salem Town. He started down the narrow dirt road and noticed that the wagon wheel ruts beneath him were narrower than he would have thought. Used to large transport trucks of his day, these ruts were proof that the means of moving freight, whether crops or other commodities, were small in comparison to what he was accustomed to.

Joshua intentionally materialized outside of town so he might get a feel for the area. Everything he was familiar with would be different. These were farming and fishing communities, neither of which Joshua knew much about. Language would be a challenge. Even though English was spoken, it hardly resembled what he was used to. He would try to speak little and listen much.

The one area in which he had an advantage was his ability to cloak his appearance. When meeting someone, or if he was with a group of people, he could project the image in their minds of whatever likeness of him he desired. He would still be in his Kalatar battle garb, but in their minds he would appear to be very appropriately dressed.

This required no active thought, and as part of his early training, it had become second nature to him. This ability would become invaluable as he would meet folks in the area with differing vocations and lifestyles. Just as a chameleon can blend in with its surroundings to avoid detection, so also would Joshua. He would blend in and hope to appear very much a part of this time period.

Joshua's game plan was to drift into Salem Town and gather as much information as he could. He would attempt to gain employment either on the waterfront near the docks or in the farming community of Salem Village. He would need to be flexible since he had no idea where he might find Corsair.

The only clue he had was the fact that Corsair had talked about sailing vessels at one time. She hadn't seemed to be the "farmer's daughter" type, so Joshua figured that near the harbor was a good place to start.

What a shame that he knew her so well…but at the same time knew so little about her earthly life. She had been secretive about it, and whenever he brought little things up, she would change the subject. It appeared she wasn't ashamed of anything, but rather expressed that she preferred to concentrate on their life and love. "Old things have passed away," she would joke, and with that, he had always felt privileged and probed no further.

The distance between Salem Village and Salem Town was about seven miles. Joshua split the difference in this stretch when he materialized so as to be near a wooded area. With all the talk of witches going around, he didn't need someone accidentally see him materializing from the spiritual into the physical.

As he walked towards town, Joshua had plenty of time to re-evaluate his situation. He knew that the enemy had at least three operatives in the area. He knew that they would probably be able to recognize him. He knew Corsair was their target, so if he encountered them he would be near her. He would need to find Corsair, gain her confidence, and convince her to follow him for her own safety.

How ironic. In the 21st century, Corsair had to convince Joshua that he had a special call on his life. It had taken time to build their relationship to a point where she could introduce him to such a wild idea…that he would battle in life and death situations for the Creator.

Now, here in the 17th century, Joshua would have to duplicate her efforts. The exception was that time could be limited. Building a relationship with her could be difficult. She might already be under attack from the enemy, and his failure would doom the future. "No pressure here," he joked to himself. With that, he suddenly realized how much he missed her. What would it be like to see her again?

🍁   🍁   🍁

The sun was bright, and no clouds interfered with it as it warmed Joshua. It was near midday now. The fog had burned off and seagulls could be seen circling overhead.

He approached a bend in the road, and as he rounded the curve he saw a sign reading "Ye Town Bridge." It was an old wooden bridge overlooking a tributary leading to the North River, and to the south he saw a body of water—a large pond. He would find out later that this pond was named "Blackford's Pond." He was troubled as he gazed upon it, but didn't know why.

Joshua stepped off the beaten path to the side of the bridge to take a little breather. Although his stamina hadn't waned, the thought of a little break was a bit appealing. A small wagon passed by as he watched from the tree line. It was hauling what appeared to be a few barrels of apples and was heading towards town.

As it bumped along the way, a few apples bounced out of the barrels and onto the road. After it was out of sight, Joshua stepped onto the road and picked up the apples. They were dried a little from their winter seclusion in a farmer's fruit cellar. "A 17th century apple," he mused.

Joshua usually saved his battle rations for emergencies, so a bit of fruit from the passing wagon would tide him over quite nicely. He could never know for sure how long it would be before he might eat again, so he decided to save his rations for later.

As he held the wrinkled red apples, one in each hand, his mind drifted back to the first time he'd shared a bit of nourishment on an operation with Corsair. "My first mission," he mused.

Thoughts of time spent with Corsair brought a smile to his face, and he reflected how much she had changed his life. A one-time self-centered salesman had become a member of an elite fighting team based in heaven itself.

"God is good," he muttered.

With that comment, Joshua's thoughts turned to his heavenly commander-in-chief. God had provided the world with a plan by which they could have eternal communion with Him. Any sacrifice Joshua might make paled in comparison to the sacrifice Christ made for all of mankind. While Joshua might contend with individual enemies of man, Jesus didn't shirk His responsibilities of taking upon Himself all the sin of mankind.

Joshua bowed his head. "Father, thank you for bringing me safe this far. Protect Corsair and give me grace in finding her. May you guide my hand against the enemies I encounter, and may you be glorified by the way I conduct myself in this era. Bless this refreshment provided by your hand. Amen."

CHAPTER 12

The Holystone Inn was an establishment that catered to sailors and dock workers in the harbor area. Whether from whalers or commercial shipping vessels, all those on shore leave found their way to the Holystone at one time or another.

The origin of its name came from a piece of sailing lore. Teaks and other wooden decks were scrubbed with a piece of sandstone, nicknamed the "holystone." It was so named because since its use always brought a man to his knees while cleaning the decks, it must be holy.

Inasmuch as the original owners worked long, hard hours to accommodate the ever hungry (and thirsty) customers, the name seemed appropriate. After a long day of meeting their needs, the workers were literally brought to their knees in cleaning up after the sometimes-rowdy sailors.

The building that housed the Holystone Inn was one of the larger buildings in town. It had been the meeting hall for Salem Town at one time. As the town grew, so did the need for a larger meeting area, and so the town leaders sold it and built a larger facility.

The old meeting house was a two-story, rectangular structure. Since the entire first floor was a former meeting hall, it was perfect for how it was now utilized. The second floor was divided into smaller rooms on each side with one hallway that ran the length of the building. Stairs at either end descended to the first floor where food and drink were abundant. Upstairs rooms could be rented for a short time to weary travelers.

Anyone who made their way up Becket Avenue from the docks to the corner of Essex Street would be able to tell right away from the sounds and smells coming from the old hall that a pleasurable time surely awaited.

The owner's name was Silas Putman, a prominent citizen whose family had been some of the original settlers who had signed the Arbella Covenant. He'd pulled a few strings to acquire the building, which housed his prosperous business. His wife Hannah served as cook, while he attended to the other aspects of the inn. Hannah always provided food known far and wide as the best you could find. Locals would be hired to help out from time to time as the need arose. When ships docked, there would always be a full house with those seeking a hot meal and a drink.

A commercial vessel was due to dock in a few days, and Silas had recently hired extra help to get things ready for the rush. William Proctor, a young lad, came to help with the cleaning of both the first and second floors.

Abigail Martin was a mother of three young children who would help serve food. Her husband John worked at the docks when ships arrived to drop off their precious cargoes. They were definitely considered working class folk but had earned the respect of the town leaders. The Martins were fine upstanding members of the church and abided by all the decisions made there.

One other woman rounded out the staff of workers. Her name was Clarisse Corsairée, a woman of French descent who worked for the Putnams on a regular basis. Her parents had died of small pox when she was a teenager, and she'd been on her own ever since. She'd worked for the Putnams for years, as well as anyone else who would offer her honest work. She always tried to keep to herself since most of the community were originally from England and there were national prejudices running deep even in this early New England town.

Clarisse was certainly considered "different" by most town folk. She seemed to know everyone, yet wasn't readily known by others. She attended church services, but always slipped in after the services started and left without spending a time of fellowship with the other believers. She was modest in dress, yet was a beautiful woman who seemed to work hard at hiding her good looks. Clarisse refused advances of single men in the community, and as far as everyone knew, she wasn't seeing anyone in secret as *was* the case with a few prominent women. Yes, Clarisse seemed to be a very proper yet mysterious member of the community. *That* would change.

CHAPTER 13

Joshua approached Salem Town from the west. As he neared, he met others who traveled in the opposite direction. They were folks who had business there and were on their way home, or others who were picking up supplies. These weren't regular farmers, but people who lived outside of town and either worked in town or had small businesses of their own.

Joshua had expected to see people dressed in what he'd thought was traditional pilgrim garb. He could remember seeing pictures of early pilgrims with hats and shoes bearing large buckles. That wasn't the case. Instead, most everyone he saw wore rather plain looking clothing that in some respects would still be recognizable today.

For men, the basic outfit might be a loose linen shirt with breeches of various styles and fabrics. Long stockings were tailored of cloth and could be knee-length or longer to fit the entire lower trunk. Common shoes were worn, but styles were shifting and boots were becoming fashionable. A felt hat and a loose fitting coat with a cape might round out a basic wardrobe.

Women, on the other hand, wore a basic undergarment much like a shirt called a shift. Over this was a corset and petticoats. On top of these clothes, she would wear an outer garment, which could be either a gown or a waistcoat, along with a skirt. An apron protected the skirt from the chores of the day. A linen cap called a coif covered her hair. Shoes, stockings, capes, and coats were much like those worn by men.

As much as Joshua wanted to hurry to find Corsair, he found himself mesmerized by the antiquity of the moment. Here he was, in a New England town, centuries before his birth, watching people going about their daily routines. He didn't look out of place, and no one gave him a second glance.

The sound of a horse-drawn wagon bearing down on him quickly brought Joshua to the reality of his moment. "Out of the way stranger!" shouted the driver. With that, the driver pulled hard to the left on the reins causing the horse to lurch to a stop, spilling the wagonload onto the roadway. Joshua moved faster than the horse to avoid a collision, but the damage was done.

Building materials of all sorts were thrown across the road. Joshua looked up at the driver with a look of apology, but the driver would have none of that.

"Who are you, the village idiot from Salem westward? Now see what you have done! Where was your mind?" He climbed down to confront Joshua.

"Sir, I'm terribly sorry, and yes, my mind was wandering. You see, I've never been to Salem Town, and I was daydreaming of what might lie ahead of me on this road. Please allow me to reload your wagon since my fault is clear in the matter."

The driver seemed to accept the explanation and looked Joshua in the eye as he introduced himself. "I'm Caleb Buffman. I own the land at the next fork in the road, where Bridge Street here turns into Essex Street."

"And I, sir, am Joshua Lunt," Joshua countered. "My family owns land up near Boxford, north of Salem Village."

"I'm not familiar with those folks," replied Caleb, "I do not follow the North River and have no business with the people of Boxford."

Hopefully my new name won't ring any bells with other folks either.

The task of reloading the wagon was strenuous work, but it was just what Joshua needed to clear his mind. The two men worked in silence except for the grunts and groans required while lifting the heavier portions of the load.

When all was complete, Joshua addressed Caleb. "If I might ask, could you please direct me to the area of the docks and where I might find a place to stay for a time?"

"Ah, my new friend, follow Essex Street east till you come to Becket Avenue. Turn towards the harbor and follow it till you come to a little jog in the street. It's at that point you'll find a reasonable boarding house run by Sarah Bartail. It's a clean place, but she'll have no rabble staying there. On past her house you'll go a short pace to the docks at Darby Street."

"My eternal thanks for your kindness and forgiveness in the matter of my clumsiness. May your day be filled with God's blessings. Good day, sir."

"And to you the same, young Joshua Lunt."

❦   ❦   ❦

Joshua was off once more, heading east on Essex Street. It was still quite a walk to his goal, but along the way he encountered an ever-increasing kaleidoscope of visuals he never could have imagined. It was like falling into a history book and becoming part of the pages. Here on every corner and in every shop he passed was a wealth of historical information.

He came to where Summer Street intersected Essex. To the south were the Southfields. It was a fair distance away according to the sign he saw on the corner. Washington Street was the next intersection. Joshua could look to the north and see indications that the town house was located nearby. An old gnarled sign showed the street was called Town House Street at one time.

On past Prison Lane, Daniel Street, and Hardy Street Joshua walked until he came to the crossing of Becket and Essex. This was quite a busy place, as traffic from the docks came north on Becket and merged with other freight moving in three directions from there.

On the corner of this intersection was an inn called Holystone. Joshua glanced through a window as he made his way south on Becket.

His first goal was to obtain gainful employment and then secure a place to stay…a base of operations per se.

To the south he walked past short, dead-end alleys and vacant buildings. The farther toward the docks he walked, the more the area seemed to take on a darker look. He did pass Sarah Bartail's boarding house, which appeared to be very well kept. However, from that point on, the area took on quite a different personality. He was moving into an area of the commercial fishing and shipping industries. This was a district where sailors and dock workers ruled.

Joshua could feel the presence of evil as he made his way toward the harbor area. God was held in low regards here. Men relied on their own strength and knowledge of the sea to get by. Superstitions ran rampant, and sailors from all points of the globe disembarked with various beliefs and religions.

Lord, guide me to the proper authority in this area. I'll need employment and proper currency to start my search.

As he rounded the next corner Joshua came upon a scene that aroused his interest. A huge man was in the process of throwing another man from the deck of a docked ship onto the pier. The sailor landed with a thud and didn't move. Another man yelled loudly as he flew over the railing of the ship and bounced from the pier and then into the water below.

"Don't return, ye scum! I need men who'll work and stay out of the bottom of a bottle of rum!" With that, the large man started down the gangplank to do further damage to the man on the dock.

Joshua stepped forward and caught the man by the arm. His strength was great, but Joshua was stronger; something the man seemed to become acutely aware of.

"They've learned their lesson surely," Joshua started. "I'm convinced that nothing more would be gained by their death."

"Who are you to tell me of my business!" he yelled. "I'll answer to no one, and certainly not you!"

"But sir, I've come to help you solve your problem…and these two have already felt your wrath this day. They will cause problems no more.

I, however, am here to offer you my services which will far surpass the efforts of these two that you have dispatched today." Joshua squeezed the arm of the man yet a little harder.

As the assailant cringed with Joshua's ever-increasing pressure, he realized a certain power and authority in Joshua. "What is your proposition, my friend?" His attitude softened as Joshua smiled.

"As I see things at this moment, you have just lost two dock workers. I'm ready and able to replace these two, providing you better service and causing you no such problems as you had with them."

"Certainly you speak a truth. By your own hand, you convince me that your strength is more than that needed to accomplish any task I set before you. You have also shown a great wisdom in this matter. I may have regretted my actions had you not stopped me. My name is Miles Ward. I run this docking area. Come with me, and I'll sign you onto the register."

Joshua followed Miles to a tiny shack off to the north side of the dock. Miles pulled an old (even by 17th century standards) dog-eared book that contained the names of all the workers and the wages to be paid. After signing up, it was agreed that Joshua would arrive early the next day to begin work.

"I would ask a courtesy of you," Joshua said. "Being new here, I have no money with which to start out fresh in Salem Town. Could you find it in your heart to favor me with an advance until my regular wages are paid?"

"Joshua Lunt, I'm not in the habit of giving money before work is performed. However, if you stop by Sarah Bartail's boarding house and tell her I sent you, you'll be able to stay there till payment for your services is doled out. And since you stayed my hand this day, I'll provide you a small amount that you might refresh yourself with a morsel or two."

"May God bless you and your business dealings for your kindness to a stranger this day," Joshua replied as he took the few coins offered to him.

"We're strangers no more Joshua Lunt. I feel we've known each other quite a while, however odd that may sound."

With that, Joshua turned and made his way toward Sarah Bartail's boarding house.

CHAPTER 14

❦

All was just as Miles had said it would be. Joshua found a room at Bartail's that would provide him a sanctuary of sorts. It was clean, neat, and simple. It had one small bed with one dresser and nightstand. One lonely candle stood vigil in the room. Sarah advised him that she would provide a bit of breakfast for her guests, but they were on their own for other nourishment for the day.

Sarah was a plump woman who appeared to be in her mid-40s. She spoke little but was quite clear with her rules. "I have only two rules here," she started. "Rule one: Pay on time or you'll find your belongings in the street. Rule two: There will be no drunkards allowed here. Drink if you must, but in moderation only, and not in my home."

Joshua assured Sarah that wouldn't be a problem, and then was off to find a meal for the evening. Hunger seemed to be his driving force at the moment. There were only a few establishments offering an evening meal, but as Joshua made his way back up Becket Avenue, he couldn't help but smell the aroma of freshly cooked food coming from the Holystone Inn.

As he neared the corner, his senses were aroused not only by the evening victuals prepared for the customers coming through the doors, but by a feeling he'd grown to know all too well. Corsair was near.

He froze in his tracks. It was unmistakable. She was near, but where? He moved forward with caution. If Corsair was near, then the enemy may be around as well. Joshua didn't sense that though. Maybe he had found her in time. He stood for a while before he reached out and turned the handle allowing the door to open and provide him with the glimpse of her that he'd waited so long to see.

The room was a hustle and bustle of people. Folks were coming and going, drinking and laughing. It reminded Joshua of pictures he had seen of saloons of the old west. People jammed around tables, laughing and talking. No strong drink was provided here, however…just great food for hungry customers.

Joshua moved slowly to a dark corner of the room and seated himself at a small table that would accommodate only two people. He sat against the wall looking out over the entire room. Corsair was nowhere to be seen. In the shadows of this corner he would be able to observe anyone entering the building.

It was just a short time before Abigail Martin presented herself before Joshua. "What may I bring you tonight, sir? We have the best stew you'll find anywhere, and if it's soup you prefer, our clam chowder is next to none."

"Stew would be fine," replied Joshua. He felt he dared not ask about Corsair. "With a cup of coffee, if you please."

"I'd be very pleased, sir. Coffee it is."

Abigail hurried off to the kitchen and Joshua could feel the nearness of Corsair. His eyes swept the room back and forth. He committed to memory the faces of each person in the room, and as newcomers, entered they got a once-over as well.

As Abigail returned from the kitchen, Joshua's heart leaped as he caught a glimpse of Corsair following closely on her heels. As Abigail moved toward him, she blocked his view and he didn't get a good look at her, but he knew at least that he had found her.

Bread and a bowl of butter were placed before Joshua, along with a steaming cup of coffee. Although simple to be sure, it was nevertheless a welcome sight. But it was Corsair he longed to see at this point, and he watched for her next entrance into the room. Abigail again approached him with his stew and left without a further word.

As the time passed, Joshua watched as Corsair made numerous trips to the kitchen and waited on all who required service. She was dressed in the garb Joshua had grown accustomed to: a simple black skirt with a white shift. Her long auburn hair was pulled into a bun and hid nicely under her coif. She seemed so innocent, and her skin appeared to be free of scars...scars she would later earn in battle.

She was five-feet, seven inches tall—slightly taller than other women of this era. As she walked around the room, her height made her easier to see. She was slender, but as she carried large trays of food to her customers, it was obvious she was stronger than she looked.

She seemed to float across the floor and appeared to be at ease around all the customers. Folks laughed and joked with her, and Joshua could tell that she worked hard to please them all. As he continued to watch, he marveled at little things she would do that he was so familiar with. It might be the way she nodded at a customer or a smile while tilting her head to one side. It was good to see her once again.

From time to time, she would glance around the room as if searching for someone...or something. Joshua realized that even now, in this time, she sensed something amiss. He knew he couldn't reveal himself to her right away, but for now it was a bit of heaven for him to see her, unhurt and well. He would need to be very careful.

He prepared to leave and paid the inn-keeper for his meal. As he headed for the door, Corsair approached in the opposite direction. Joshua was like a teenager with a crush on a high school cheerleader. His blood rushed to his face and he looked away as her eyes met his. *That was enough, just a glance into her eyes.* She stopped in her tracks and lingered, blocking his path. Then finally, "Excuse me, kind sir," as she stepped out of his way and he passed without a word.

He was speechless, but that was probably best. There was no denying though that Corsair felt a pull, much like Joshua had felt when he first set eyes on her in the distant future. Now, the mystery was with Joshua—it *was* Joshua. Who was this mysterious man?

❋   ❋   ❋

Joshua spent the rest of the evening from a distance, his gaze on the Holystone. He not only wanted to be near Corsair, but to protect her as she left the inn. So he waited, in the shadows, as darkness fell.

When Corsair finally left for the evening, she headed north across Essex on Becket. Joshua followed from a distance. Normally, another mortal would have no idea they were being followed, but Joshua wanted to take extra care to remain hidden from Corsair. Although he was skilled in the art of stealth, she might sense his presence if he came too close.

Corsair continued north past a section of common land. It was common in the sense that no one had claimed this parcel of land as his own. It was of no value for any endeavor. The land was rocky near town and then became even more desolate the farther north you traveled until you ended up in a swampy area.

Corsair turned down a narrow path long before coming to the swamp. Joshua lost sight of her in the darkness but relied on his training and other senses to follow. She seemed to know exactly her destination and followed the narrow pathway as if she had traveled this way many times.

After a few minutes, the short journey ended as the path led to a little clearing, and in the clearing a small shack. Joshua watched as she made her way to the door. A slight pause and a glance over her shoulder, and Corsair disappeared from sight. A kerosene lantern illuminated the inside, and curtains were drawn tight for the night.

Joshua sighed as he whispered, "So this is your earthly home, my beloved. I pray we'll succeed in this mission so you and I may be together once again in God's glorious kingdom."

CHAPTER 15

The next morning, Sarah Bartail was true to her word. Up before dawn, she prepared a small but tasty bit of breakfast for her boarders. At the present time, only three others shared the table with Joshua. Hot coffee, eggs, bacon, and homemade bread were in abundance.

Those around the table talked of the weather and other news of the day—whether rumor or fact. The weather was turning cold again, being as it was still March. The early spring-like weather had spoiled all of Salem Town. A harbor town never really relaxed concerning the weather until summer set in.

"I hear another witch was arrested evening last," said one man.

"Mrs. Bartail, how many is that now?" asked another.

"Lord, I know not. My boarders keep me too busy to concern myself with talk of devils and witches. I only know for sure what takes place here in my house, so I'll have no more talk of that!"

"Even so," added the third, "It's enough to trouble the soul. I've heard that Sarah Good and Sarah Osborne were taken and jailed in Boston."

The first boarder responded. "Why, that's old news, my friend. That happened weeks ago. I do believe though that Rebecca Nurse was taken into custody the other day."

"Not Rebecca! That old woman wouldn't hurt a soul," added Mrs. Bartail. Even though she wanted no part of this conversation, she couldn't resist giving her opinion on the arrests. "I'll also tell you that they had no business taking Sarah Good's daughter, Dorcas, into custody. Jail is no place for a four-year-old girl!"

"What think you of these things, young man?" asked the first boarder.

Joshua thought long before he answered. "I think it best to dwell on God's goodness and remember He has power over the forces of evil."

"Rightly so," all agreed, though it may not have been the answer they expected.

With that, they finished their meals and all went about their duties of the day.

❦   ❦   ❦

Joshua headed toward the docks with his thoughts still on his brief encounter with Corsair. *She's more beautiful than I remember. How will I ever convince her that she's in danger?*

He thought about simply kidnapping her, an easy task in this era. But he quickly abandoned the idea. If Satan's operatives were left alone in this century, who knows what havoc they could create? That alone could alter the future. No, he must see this through to the end, whatever dangers that might entail.

As he neared the docks, the sun was just peeking over the horizon. The air was brisk and seagulls circled overhead looking for a morning snack. There was a lot of hustle and bustle as men hurried here and there moving cargo around the dock area.

A new ship had arrived, and the day would be long and hard as the men emptied the ship's hold of its precious cargo. There would be few breaks allowed during the day, as Miles was ever present to keep the men working the block and tackles as cargo was hoisted from the ship to the docks and then onto freight wagons bound for their final destinations.

Some sailors on the deck would throw insults at the dock workers when they thought the work wasn't progressing with the speed they thought it should. Their main interests weren't in accomplishing the task for the ship's captain, but in accomplishing the task so they might be done early and disembark for an evening of revelry.

Joshua worked hard, but while he worked he became aware of a dark presence on the ship. One huge sailor, in particular, sparked his interest. Two others were near at hand, and the three seemed out of place with the other ship hands. "I'll have to keep an eye on those three," Joshua grunted as he lifted another heavy load.

The day finally came to an end, and the dock workers lined up for their daily pay. Miles was extremely glad that he had hired Joshua. "Your promise was good my friend. You did truly provide me a better value than the two you replaced. I'll see you again tomorrow."

Joshua turned to leave, and as he turned he bumped into the huge sailor he'd seen earlier in the day.

"Out of my way, you country bumpkin! Make way for a real man!" And with that, he gave Joshua a shove that would have toppled most men. Joshua, however, pretended to be caught unaware and fell backwards a step or two as the three men continued on laughing at the encounter.

"Joshua!" Miles stammered. "Why did you permit that? I know your strength. I know you could have brought him to his knees in great agony. Now he thinks you less a man for this."

"Miles, it is best for now for him to believe just that. I believe we'll see more of him. I sense a bit of evil surrounding those three. It's a wise man for sure who feels no need to impress others with his strength. For now, for tonight, we'll be the wise men here on this dock." With that, Joshua walked away.

❦   ❦   ❦

Joshua rushed back to the Bartail's to clean up a bit. Sarah had left soap, towels, and a pitcher of water on his dresser next to a large bowl. After washing the dirt and sweat of the day from his body, he was ready to head for the Holystone for dinner once more.

He paid Sarah for her hospitality and agreed to a weekly rate. He was out the door and heading up Becket Avenue.

The inn was a beehive of activity as sailors from the new ship crowded in. Joshua found his table in the corner and settled in, looking forward to a hearty meal.

As he looked about the room, he was caught unaware as his server for the evening approached from his blind side. "How may I serve you this fine evening, sir?"

It was Corsair. Joshua's heart froze. He looked around to see her standing before him. He wanted to leap from his chair and embrace her. He wanted to hold her in his arms and proclaim his undying love for her. He wanted to whisper "I love you" in her ear. But he knew he couldn't. That would have to wait.

Before he realized what he was saying, he blurted out, "Good evening, my Corsair. It's truly good to see you tonight."

"Kind sir, you seem to know a bit about me, but only in part. I would have thought you might get my name correct if you would care to address me personally. A corsair is a sailing vessel. For your information tonight, my name is Clarisse Corsairée.

"Clarisse," Joshua breathed. "Of course."

She looked him in the eyes, and Joshua felt as he had the first time their eyes met. This time, he knew she was experiencing the same thing.

"Corsairée, that has a French sound to it," he added.

The attraction was strong as she answered, "That would be correct, sir."

Someone yelled for Clarisse to hurry to help other customers, which brought her (and Joshua) back to reality. She took his order and was off. She smiled warmly as she turned to leave.

Well, that went well.

Clarisse came and went. She served not only Joshua but also a multitude of people. When she had the opportunity, she would glance in Joshua's direction. If he caught her gaze, she would blush and turn away.

So my darling Corsair is a bit shy. That's different. Joshua's mind drifted to the battles they'd had and the confrontations with demonic spirits. She was anything but shy and was unrelenting in her pursuit to destroy the Creator's enemies. For now, he would enjoy learning more about this bashful Clarisse.

As Joshua was finishing his meal, the doors opened and some rather loud and boisterous voices were heard. In walked the sailor and his two friends Joshua had encountered earlier that day. It appeared that they had been somewhere else earlier that evening because they all had the look of those who had been drinking.

They swaggered across the room, pushing through the crowd as they went, and took a table close to Joshua. Joshua moved his chair a few inches back into the shadows and decided to watch them a while.

They laughed aloud and made fun of some of the "land lovers" and the way they were dressed. Clarisse came by to take their order and they made it difficult for her to do her job.

As she returned with their drinks, they complained loudly that there was no strong drink at the Holystone. Silas Putman came out of the kitchen and firmly recommended the men leave if they wanted something other than what was served. They laughed as he turned to leave. "Food! Bring us our food so we may partake and leave this hole in the wall!"

As Clarisse walked by serving other guests, the ringleader of the three tried several times to grab her. At first she was caught unaware, but then tried to avoid that area of the room. When it was time to serve their table, she approached with caution.

As she set the food on the table, huge hands gripped her around the waist and drew her close. She slapped the sailor in the face, which only made him more aggressive. All three laughed and Clarisse let out a small scream. No one in the room moved to help. Sensing approval from the crowd, the sailor became more forward and tried to force his hand under her skirt.

As the room became silent, Joshua rose from his chair and slipped silently to the table. "I believe this woman would have none of your advances!" his voice boomed in the old meeting hall. "You'll remove your hands from her at once!"

Now the room was absolutely silent. No one dared breathe. All was quiet, save the slight whimper that escaped the lips of Clarisse. The huge man just looked at Joshua as an evil grin spread across his bearded face. "Why, it's the country bumpkin! Here to save the fair maiden?" he asked sarcastically as he squeezed Clarisse closer to his body.

Joshua moved with lightning speed. With one blow to the throat and two quick kicks to his associates' chests, the attackers were rendered helpless and writhing in agony. Others in the room finally came to their senses and took charge of dispatching the rowdies from the Holystone.

Joshua took Clarisse by the hand and led her back toward his table. She was shaken for sure, but intrigued by her rescuer. "Sir, a debt I owe you this night. You seem to have made a few enemies in the short time you have been among us. I'll pray for your protection from those who would do you great harm."

"Clarisse, by your own words, you owe a debt to me. I request payment tonight that I may walk you to your door so that no further harm would come to you."

"Sir, you know not what you ask. I'm but a poor girl and live apart from the good townsfolk of Salem."

"That's all the more reason to watch over you. I'll plead with you again that tonight is the best time for you to pay your debt to me. I'll wait nearby for you answer." With that, Joshua rose from the table and left.

❦   ❦   ❦

Joshua waited in the shadows. All was quiet as Clarisse departed the Holystone. She stopped before stepping across the street, looking back and forth. She could have been looking for her assailants…or her rescuer. She pulled a shawl from her shoulders up and over her head. The night was cold and her pace was quick.

Joshua stepped from the shadows and followed silently behind. When he couldn't stand it any longer he softly said, "My dear Clarisse, I still await your answer."

She turned with a start, but knew who this was. Her response surprised Joshua. "Sir, you do not know me well enough to address me with such an affectionate tone. Though you seem to think you know me, I know not even your name."

"Forgive me, Clarisse. I meant no disrespect. My name is Joshua, Joshua Lunt. However, we stand here in the cold while we could be a few steps closer to your home. Do I have the honor of escorting you this night?"

She smiled as she considered this prospective suitor. Although he wasn't traditionally handsome, there was an attractive quality about him. His brown hair was shorter than she was used to seeing, and his features were rugged in an unusual way. His eyes were captivating, and although he was only a head taller than her, it was apparent that he was quite capable of handling himself in a fight.

"Joshua. That's not a very angelic name," she responded. "I would have thought your name might be Gabriel, like the angel. You *have* been my guardian this day."

"You may consider me an angel, then," he replied as his mind raced back to his first dinner with Corsair. When confronted, she had responded in kind, "I'm what you might consider an angel."

They walked in silence for a time. When they came to the narrow pathway leading to her tiny shack, she stopped. "You may go your own way now, my angel. There's no need for you to continue on."

"I would be a slacker if I stopped anywhere but at your door."

"But my dwelling is meager at best. I wish you not to see any further up this pathway."

"Clarisse, please." With that, he took her hand in his and pulled her along toward her home, hands clasped. Once there, he walked her to the door, held her hand up, and gently kissed it. "Your debt is now paid. Good night, Clarisse Corsairée."

He turned and disappeared into the evening.

CHAPTER 16

❦

March gave way to April and Joshua's days would become filled with routine: up early and off to the docks where he would have a full day of backbreaking work; after that, a visit to the Holystone, and the day would end with a watchful eye on Clarisse.

The two were becoming fast friends. Clarisse had never felt a part of the community, being of French descent. Joshua was still considered an outsider. No one knew him or the "Lunt family." So they felt drawn together as two strangers in a foreign land, enjoying their mutual alienation from the community in general.

They were careful not to display any public signs of affection (to Joshua's dismay). The Puritan ideals of the day would frown on any outward show of endearment. So Joshua would settle for a growing friendship and a developing bond with Clarisse for right now.

Those who worked with Clarisse daily could see that she seemed to be much happier. It didn't escape their notice that the stranger from Boxford was now a regular each day, keeping a close eye on her. Other regulars at the Holystone Inn whispered about his true intents. Gossip was a true art form for those with no other type of entertainment.

Weeks went by with no further sign of trouble. Joshua was spending some of his time away from the docks scouting the town. He became familiar with most of the streets and alleyways.

One area in particular was near the town's meeting house. About a block away was an area called "the commons." This was a place where townsfolk would gather at times and discuss the news of the day or have a platform to debate issues in an open forum. What made this place different from the meeting hall was that women were allowed to speak in this open venue. Inside the meeting hall only men were allowed to speak—and then only when called upon. It was the meeting hall where trials were conducted for folks who might break one of the many rules of Church or State.

It was early in April as Joshua made one of his visits to the commons area to hear what might be happening in Salem Town. Spring was in the air, and with the warmer weather upon them, folks gathered to discuss the previous week's events.

A public fast had been declared on March 31, 1692, in response to that month's frenzy of accusations and arrests. After the original arrests of Sarah Osborne, Sarah Good, and Tituba in the first week of March, the town had been buzzing with talk of all that'd been going on in Salem Village.

Martha Corey was jailed on March 21st, and all were amazed when Dorcus Good, Sarah's young daughter, was arrested on the 23rd.

Reverend Samuel Parris of the Salem Village church declared on March 27th, "The devil hath been raised among us." And so a public fast was called for March 31.

Joshua was interested that a larger than normal crowd had gathered, and he made his way to a good vantage point on the fringe of the area. One woman was in the middle of a discourse as Joshua came within earshot.

"Rebecca Nurse is no more a witch than the pastor's wife!"

"Careful what you say there, good woman, that you may not be associated with her. Sara Holton was quite positive about her accusation."

"I tell you that the woman is 71 years old. She would do no person here any harm!"

One after another, the comments came fast and furious.

"I know her husband and his family. There is none more kind and generous than they are. We have all done business with him and found him to be most honest."

"I hear her sisters are under suspicion as well!"

"Trash, all of you! We all know that this good woman has been steadfast and simple in heart. She loves her church and her community!"

"What better disguise than to be among the righteous. A wolf in sheep's clothing to be sure!"

Finally, a person was loud enough to be heard above the rest. "I have here a petition. It's a petition in support of this dear woman. I would urge all you good folk to sign it!"

With that, Joshua felt it a good time to leave the area. Things were heating up in this community, and he could feel a cloud of darkness begin to settle in.

🍁 🍁 🍁

The next day, a newly arrived ship was docked and ready for the workers to unload. Each man on the dock knew their place and the work went smoothly. The sailors participated on board keeping the cranes delivering heavy loads one after another.

They were almost finished when Joshua noticed one of the sailors on deck was the one he'd had a confrontation with at the Holystone. He eyed Joshua from the deck, but hurled no insults in his direction as before.

So, you're back. Tonight I'll keep an eye on you. A slight shiver ran up his spine as he watched him.

At the end of the day, with the work completed, the workers would file past the pay window once more. Joshua lagged behind near the end of the line to watch for any signs of trouble.

The huge sailor filed down the gangplank and past Joshua without a single word. The air was thick with anticipation. What bothered Joshua was that the sailor gave a cruel smile as he made his exit from the docks.

As Joshua left, he asked another sailor the name of the man. "Why, that be John Collins; and I'd stay out of his way if I were you! He singled you out to be on his list of things to take care of tonight!"

"I thank you for that information. I will take care to be on business elsewhere this night."

"That would be wise, my friend. Collins is one man you don't want as an enemy."

With that, the two men went their separate ways. Joshua hurried up Becket Avenue and arrived at the Holystone earlier than normal. Clarisse waved as he entered and he settled into his favorite chair in the corner. Few people were there yet, and Clarisse came by to take his order.

"What may I get you this fine evening, my angel?"

"Nothing tonight, Clarisse. It appears there may be trouble brewing this evening. I'd ask you to take care and keep a watchful eye. Your former antagonist is near; his name appears to be John Collins. We'll be on guard to see what distress is stirring."

Clarisse nodded, but smiled and said, "He'd be a fool to engage you again."

"You believe that to be true, but I tell you a truth, there are powerful forces of evil lurking about that you know not. I would wish you never know, but you will soon have more knowledge of good and evil than ever before. I pray you will continue to trust God and how He leads us."

"You speak in riddles this night," she responded, her expression growing somber.

"Clarisse, I only wish a riddle was all we had to unravel tonight. Pray even as you go about your duties."

🍁　　🍁　　🍁

The room was filled once more with hungry people, mostly men from the docked ships. Joshua continued to watch and wait. About two hours before the time of closing John Collins walked in with the other two scoundrels following close behind. They made no commotion as they chose a table near the door.

Abigail waited on them and they quietly talked among themselves. Collins glanced in Joshua's direction a number of times and continued to sneer at him as if he knew something Joshua didn't.

Joshua grew continually uneasy. He felt a growing sense of foreboding and premonition of danger in the air. He couldn't put his finger on it, but Collins was too composed. It was as if he were waiting for something to happen.

The evening wore on. People came and went. The three by the door had their dinner and finally left, laughing as they went. It was near the time of closing, and Joshua became more assured than ever that danger was at hand. He could feel it in the air. All of his senses were at heightened alert.

Clarisse came to his table with a look of concern on her face. She could tell that Joshua sensed something amiss. "Clarisse, whatever happens, if we become separated this night, I want you to run as fast as you can to your home and wait for me there."

"Joshua, what is it? What's wrong?"

"Ask no questions now, all will become clear later. Just, please, do as I ask. There is evil brewing tonight."

As Clarisse turned to leave Joshua felt the very presence of evil in the spirit realm nearby. As he looked around the room, his attention was drawn to the stairway leading up to the second floor of the inn. Halfway up the stairs was a demon that turned and motioned for Joshua to follow. No one else could see this apparition of death save Joshua. He knew immediately that this was his first 21st century opponent.

He became focused on one thing as he left his seat and headed for the stairs. It was the total destruction of this first adversary he'd meet in this era. The specter disappeared as Joshua hurried to engage it. Up the stairs he bounded and reached the second floor only to find an empty hallway.

With eyes focused on the spiritual realm, Joshua found his prey, and without a moment's thought, he popped out of the material and into the ethereal venue of combat. Now all pretenses were dropped. This wasn't Joshua Lunt, 17th century laborer, overmatched and outgunned. This was a member of heaven's mighty Order of Kalatar. The mightiest fighters ever assembled.

Joshua now faced his opponent as they both rose through ceiling and roof. This particular demon was neither large in stature nor hideous to the eye. In fact, it would appear to be very attractive to a mortal who might encounter it. But Joshua wasn't fooled by it's seemingly lack of intimidating qualities. He was quite aware of its deadly nature. Its sole purpose, at the moment, was the complete and utter destruction of Joshua.

They continued upward into the atmosphere above Salem Town. Their gazes were locked onto each other as they, each in their own way, looked for a weakness to exploit.

Joshua drew his sword and it flamed bright as he held it high above his head. His adversary wasn't alarmed in the least. Joshua could sense that this ghoul had engaged members of The Order before.

Reaching from behind its back it produced a flaming ball of fire in each hand. With an unholy screech that shattered the surrounding heavens, it hurled the fiery spheres toward Joshua. As it did so, it turned and raced further upward into the firmament of the air, further from Salem Town.

With lightning speed, Joshua deflected the first and then the other ball of fire with his sword. Without a second thought, he hastened after the demon. He didn't want to lose this chance to eliminate one of the enemy forces from the future.

CHAPTER 17

❀

Clarisse didn't see were Joshua went. She assumed he had left to follow Collins. With nothing else to do for the evening, she prepared to leave for the night. Joshua's words rang in her ears as she hurried out and into the darkness. Quick were her steps and vigilant her eyes as she watched for danger.

As she hurried across Essex Street, she felt as if there were eyes upon her. She glanced over her shoulder and thought she saw someone disappear into the shadows. She picked up her pace, and her breathing became a bit labored. The street was void of any traffic and fear came over her.

Now Clarisse could hear footsteps behind her as she made her way further on Becket. Panic was beginning to set in, and she broke out into a run as she turned up the narrow path to her home. Behind her, in the distance, she heard an evil laugh, and it caused her heart to pound even more. Her stalker seemed to stop from the sound of it, but she took no chances and ran even harder for her porch and the safety of her home.

Up the three stairs of her front porch and through the door she flew. Once inside, she turned to face the door and slid the bolt into place. Now she could breathe a little easier. She was safe…or so she thought.

Clarisse turned in the darkened room. She could sense that something was wrong, very wrong. "Who's here?" she whispered. There was no answer.

From somewhere deep inside, Clarisse shook the fear from her soul and gathered the courage to speak again. "I don't know who you are or what you want, but you are not welcome here. You will leave at once!"

Then…a deep, evil chuckle. A match was lit, and the dim illumination it gave revealed the ugly facial features of John Collins as he lit a cigar. "There'll be no rescue for you this time, my French whore. We'll see if you can be friendlier tonight."

At first, Clarisse was frozen with fear. She had no illusions to what Collins was implying. Her mind whirled as thoughts came at lightning speed. She surprised herself with concern for Joshua instead of herself. *Where is he? He must be hurt. Did this animal harm him? What am I to do?*

"What have you done with my friend?"

"He's of no concern to you now. He is presently having a few problems of his own to deal with. He'll not come to bother us, I assure you. I would think you should worry about your own life and how to save it."

With that he quickly rose from where he was seated and moved across the room. Clarisse turned and fumbled with the sliding latch on the door, but Collins was on her before she could unlock the door. He grabbed her by the arm and hurled her away from the door to the opposite side of the room.

Then, he rushed over and grabbed her before she knew what was happening. He pulled her close, and Clarisse could smell the filth that Collins wore like a cloak. His breath made her want to vomit. As he tried to kiss her, she reached up with a free hand and raked her fingernails across his bearded face.

He screamed as he stepped back, his face bleeding from the four deep scratches. "You wench! You'll pay for that!" He punched her in the face and she fell backwards, bleeding from the nose.

He reached once more to grab her. Her speed was no match for his, and she found herself trapped again as they wrestled together on the floor. This time his huge body pinned her to the hearth.

Clarisse's mind became a blur. She couldn't believe this was happening. Collins tore at her clothing, and before she knew it, he had ripped her top, exposing her breasts.

In the darkness, she reached for whatever weapon she could find. Her hand came to rest on the fireplace poker. With all the force she could muster, she brought it to bear on her assailant. She swung upward from the prone position and found her mark.

Although it wasn't enough to disable Collins, he rolled off to one side, giving her an opportunity to get to the door. As quickly as possible, she unlocked the door and bounded out into the night. She didn't get far however.

Collins' two accomplices were waiting there according to his instructions. It was his plan to be alone with Clarisse. Now these two became his back-up plan. They grabbed Clarisse and wrestled her to the ground.

Collins emerged from the cabin in rage. Bleeding now from new wounds to his head, he made his way to where Clarisse was being held down. He stepped up to her and kicked her in the ribs. Clarisse heard bones crack as the pain shot through her body.

Then the huge fists came raining down, one after another. All found their mark as the other two joined in the torture. Her face became a bloody pulp, her body twisted and broken. She was near blacking out as she felt her clothes being torn off one layer at a time.

Clarisse willed her mind to be alert. From somewhere deep inside, she knew it was important she keep fighting—if not physically, then mentally. *These animals must not win! I must fight till Joshua comes!*

Collins seemed to grow weary of the continuing abuse these three were inflicting and brought his attention back to the original purpose of his visit. As Clarisse lay before him broken, bruised, and naked, he stood over her with all of the calm he had when she entered her cabin.

Stationary over her and with his two conspirators holding her down, he slowly undid the clasp on his breeches. Clarisse was barely conscious, but she saw the intent of Collins.

Now a new battle would be waged. Collins forced himself onto her. This new assault awakened her senses even more. She wouldn't give in willingly. With each thrust of his massive body, she gained new strength knowing this invasion of her body was temporal. The greater battle was spiritual. He would not defeat her.

As Collins finished his assault, his breathing became less labored, and he drew close to Clarisse in exhaustion. She took this opportunity for one last counter attack. With all the strength she could muster, she raised her head to his ear and bit down as hard as she could.

Collins screamed in agony, and as he pulled away, his ear was ripped from his head. Blood poured from the wound as he rolled around in pain. The two other fiends were shocked that Clarisse could muster an assault in her weakened condition.

It may have been her last effort because the beatings began again with renewed vigor.

CHAPTER 18

It seemed too easy, Joshua thought, as he quickly caught up with his retreating foe. After the chase ended, the battle seemed to deteriorate into a series of mini attacks and retreats. Joshua would attack; the demon would counter and then run. This series of retreats troubled Joshua. *This demon is more powerful than this. Why won't he fight?*

With each retreat the demon seemed more pleased with itself. Joshua grew more and more frustrated. He felt like the proverbial mule with a carrot dangling in front of it. It was at this point that he remembered the evil grin he had seen on Collins' face earlier that evening.

"Clarisse!" he shouted. And with that he turned to rush back to earth. As he turned to leave, the enemy behind him suddenly attacked in earnest. *Now I see! This demon was just a distraction!*

The battle now took a violent turn. Joshua was hit in the back with a bolt of lightning from the fingertips of the ghoul. He tumbled head over heels and righted himself in time to dodge another. One after another they came. Some missed him, some were deflected, and some found their mark.

Joshua grew weak as he was battered with all the fury and power a bolt of lightning could carry. Only his protective clothing saved him from being incinerated. One salvo after another brought him to his knees. He knew he had to dispatch this enemy quickly if he had any hope of getting to Clarisse.

In a moment of desperation, he retracted the flaming blade and looked his adversary in the eye. Victory seemed to favor his enemy. With an evil smile spreading wide across its face, the demon drew back for one final volley, then let fly with an enormous bolt of lightning.

Joshua flipped his sword around and grasped it by the short steel blade. The hilt, facing upward and toward the enemy, took the brunt of the blast. As the bolt continued from the fingertips of the demon to the hilt of the sword, the energy was absorbed by Joshua's weapon. The insignia of the Kalatar began to glow white-hot, and the sword shook in his hands.

Just when he thought he couldn't hold on any longer, a gigantic blast shook the firmament and an enormous flash of energy retreated from the Kalatar emblem toward the demon. In an instant, the enemy was vaporized as all the energy used to attack Joshua was redirected back to its source.

Now getting back to Clarisse was vital. With this enemy destroyed, he could sense that Clarisse was really in trouble. "How could I've been so stupid? I should have remembered that *she* was the target!"

With that he immediately made his way back to Salem Town. Speeding through the firmament at lightning speed, it was only a matter of seconds until he burst into the material world. When he did, he was horrified at what he saw.

There on the ground, stripped and exposed, lay Clarisse, held down and being beaten by two men. Collins was reeling backward as if attacked by some unseen forces. Screaming, and with blood pouring from his face and head, he reversed his direction and moved toward Clarisse once more. As he did so, he reached to the side of his boot and pulled out a large knife.

Rushing toward Clarisse, Joshua burst into the natural realm and chose to reveal himself as he truly was, a Kalatar warrior. The sound of his exploding onto the scene, and his appearance, caused all three attackers to recognize the fact that they were in serious trouble.

With one sweeping arc of his flaming blade, he separated Collins' right arm from his body. The other two were so horrified at the scene and at Collins' screams that they turned to run. It only took two steps to block one of them, and Joshua took his anger out on him. Once more the flaming sword met flesh and this mortal was cut in half. He let loose a blood-curdling scream as he viewed his lower torso lying a few feet from his upper.

The third thought he'd gotten away as the screams retreated to his rear. He ran through thicket and briars until he came to an opening that approached a swampy area. With nowhere to run, he moved to some slimy, moss-covered fallen trees to hide. As he tried to bury himself deep in the bog, he trembled when he heard someone speak.

"You cannot hide! You'll now pay for your transgressions this night!" With that, a razor-sharp steel blade entered his back, and, piercing his heart, he died without a sound.

Joshua now returned his attention to Collins, who was still writhing in pain at the feet of Clarisse. The flame had cauterized the wound at the same time it had separated arm from body. He walked over to Collins and with one hand grasping him by the throat, lifted him up and pinned him against a nearby tree.

"Who sent you here?" he screamed.

Collins croaked, "I can't breathe!"

Joshua allowed him to hang there a bit longer then dropped him to the ground. He drew his blade once more. It burst into flame at his command, and Collins screamed again as the white-hot heat extending from the hilt neared his remaining arm.

"Who sent you here? I'll not ask again!"

Collins was reduced to a blubbering mass of flesh as he responded, "Alright, enough! I'll tell you!"

"Who then? And what were you told to do? What was your mission?"

"We were told to attack and kill this wench!"

With that term used to describe Clarisse, Joshua brought a boot down hard on Collins' throat. "You'll speak no more of her in those terms! I'll allow you to live only if it suits me. Answer and live…remain silent and die!"

"They will kill me if I reveal to you what you ask!"

"Then you sign your own death warrant by remaining silent! Tell me what I wish and you have a small chance of surviving!"

Collins was terrified. Whoever sent him had instilled a deep fear of failure in him. But Joshua was the present danger now. He appeared to consider his options then responded, "The one who sent me is a powerful man in Salem. He is known by the name...."

It was his last utterance. Collins was pierced through the neck and heart with demonic arrows from above. Death was instantaneous. With the deed done, the two assassins looked at Joshua in horror. They sensed immediately that he was more powerful than the Kalatar they were used to.

They turned to attack Clarisse, but Joshua had already sensed their intent and blocked the next volley by stepping in front of her. The arrows fell harmlessly off of his trench coat.

These two were demons of this era that Joshua was told he might encounter. With lightning speed and superior skills, Joshua caught them and crushed the unholy life from them with little trouble. He threw their miserable bodies next to Collins' where they promptly crumbled to dust.

Had these two even a spark of a brain between them, they would have attacked Clarisse first. But these simple minions were trained to follow orders, and the order given them was to silence Collins. Joshua considered luck on his side. He had let his emotions dictate his actions when he should have protected Clarisse first and foremost.

With the action over with, he turned his attention now to Clarisse. Her naked body was bruised and battered. Her face was a bloody pulp, and her breathing labored and sporadic. Her ribs were caved in and Joshua wept as he saw that Collins had taken her sexually.

He retrieved a blanket from the cabin and wrapped her in it. It was paramount in his mind to get her medical help even in this primitive time period. She needed someone to tend to her wounds, and as he lifted her in his arms she opened her eyes and focused on him.

"My angel has come at last. I knew you would."

"I am sorrowful that I was not in time to prevent this."

"Joshua, I didn't give in. I didn't stop fighting."
"I know, my dearest, I know." And with that she lost consciousness.

🍁   🍁   🍁

Joshua made his way back to town carrying Clarisse in his arms. He weaved his way through the back streets of Salem Town that he had come to know so well. His goal was to get Clarisse to a doctor without being seen. It was important to not be associated with the happenings in and around the swamp this night.

As he stood in front of the door where the doctor lived, he once more cloaked his appearance. The doctor's wife came to the door, and she let out a gasp when she saw the condition of Clarisse. All she could see of Joshua was the hidden form of a man in a hooded cloak.

Dr. Browne rushed into the room and helped carry her into the back part of his office. As he examined her, Joshua turned so the light revealed nothing about his appearance. Taking a leather pouch from an inner pocket, he laid it down on the table.

"There is more than enough here to cover your costs in ministering to her needs," Joshua remarked. "Rest assured that the scoundrels responsible for this have been taken care of. I pray for your skills in attending to Clarisse…I bid you farewell." He turned, walked out the door, and disappeared into the night.

Joshua knew he would be more alert now of further attempts. He berated himself for being lax and caught off-guard. It wouldn't happen again.

With Clarisse in the hands of the doctor, Joshua made his way back to her cabin. He would need to take care of Collins and his friends. He couldn't afford to leave evidence around for the authorities to find.

As he returned to the scene of the attack, he quickly found a shovel in a shed behind the house. After removing their leather pouches of gold coins (they would have no use of these), he set out at once to bury the three bodies deep in the swamp. It didn't take long to erase any evidence of Collins having been there…and with one last look around, he headed back to town.

CHAPTER 19

❀

In the early days of May, Joshua visited with Clarisse regularly. The doctor's wife, Martha, was always warm and friendly to him when he'd visit. The doctor had treated Clarisse's wounds as best he could, but the damage was severe.

Joshua would visit during the day and was an unseen sentry at night. Sleep would come, but only in short intervals. He wasn't working at the docks now but chose to remain close at hand in case the enemy would try another attack.

The rumors at the Holystone Inn ran rampant. The story of Clarisse being attacked was common knowledge, but there were no suspects. The shadowy character that had left her with the doctor was specific that the attackers were taken care of, but whom could he have meant, and who was he?

There appeared to be no one missing, but with the ships in and out of the harbor each week, it would be difficult to keep track of everyone. The authorities didn't seem to want to spend a lot of time investigating the attack. To them, Clarisse was still considered an outsider. Their investigation was token at best.

As the time drew near for her release from the doctor's care, Clarisse grew more uneasy. Joshua noticed that she had become more sullen and hardly spoke at all. Although they knew her recovery would be lengthy, it seemed something else concerned her.

Joshua waited for a time when they were alone to see if he might find an answer to what was troubling her. "Clarisse," he asked gently, "you seem to be disturbed these last few days. Are we not about to take you home? I would think that would lift your spirits."

It took her time to gather the courage to respond, but when she did, it wasn't the answer Joshua had expected. "Lift my spirits?! Do you even realize what you are suggesting? You want to take me back to the place of my shame! How could I ever go back there? What kind of a world do we live in that allows the likes of John Collins to roam the city and ruin lives? Why would God allow such a thing to happen? I do not feel I can ever return home again!"

Joshua was shocked. In his zeal to protect her, he had never even considered the psychological damage inflicted upon her. He took her hand in his and tried his best to comfort her.

"I'm so sorry, Clarisse, that I have not been mindful of your distress. I am realizing now how hard this ordeal has been. Please forgive me for my thoughtlessness. Is there something we might do to calm your fears?"

"I know nothing that would heal my spirit," she said, looking toward the floor. "I feel as though a part of me has died."

Joshua thought for a minute and suggested, "Is it possible that we might find a haven at the Holystone? It would be a place where you would be welcomed and well taken care of."

"Is that the answer to this dilemma? That I may never go home again? I know that my cabin is small, but it's all I have in this world…and now it's a place of dread and fear for me!"

With that comment, Joshua felt a tug in his heart and knew what he needed to share with Clarisse. "Clarisse, I feel the Lord would have me reveal a truth to you. He knows the pain you feel this day, and He's aware that you have suffered more than most will ever be called on to endure. I tell you a truth that in the weeks ahead, you'll learn more about the dangers we'll face together in the near future."

Even as he spoke, his mind raced 400 years in the future to a time when Corsair would utter similar words to him. He now took both of her hands in his and looked her in the eyes. "Clarisse, whether it's a healing for your body, or a healing from the fears that assail you now, the Lord wants you to know that His grace is sufficient for your needs. His grace and mercy endure forever. They will continue on long after the John Collinses of the world are gone. He will help us to overcome even this!"

As Clarisse listened, she felt an unusual peace come upon her. She could see in Joshua's eyes the truth in the words he spoke, and even the mention of future dangers caused no alarm. She sensed a call to trust his words and believed that somehow things would be all right.

She almost whispered her response, "Yes, your words ring true. I feel a sense of peace about me as you speak. Although it will be difficult to overcome, I will pray for the strength that God will provide. His mercy is great. Thank you Joshua."

🍁 🍁 🍁

About a week and a half later, the doctor reluctantly allowed Clarisse to leave his care. Joshua arranged for a wagon to pick her up, and, very carefully, she was transported back to her home. Joshua prepared things at the cabin so she could be as comfortable as possible.

As the wagon turned onto the narrow lane leading to her home, Joshua could sense the growing anxiety of Clarisse. She held onto his arm tighter, and he could feel her begin to shake.

He ordered to driver to stop and let them off. "We'll walk the rest of the way." With that said, the man was paid, and he turned his team around to head back to town.

"I'm scared," she whispered.

"Clarisse, let's pray. The Lord will give us the strength we need." Taking a moment, he kneeled with her by a large oak tree and began: "Precious Lord, hear us today as we lift our voices to you. Clarisse, your servant, needs strength from you at this time. She needs grace once more to confront this fear that intends to bind her. Please bless her again so she might bear witness to your awesome power. May she serve you as never before from this day forward. Amen."

As they stood together, the fear left Clarisse once again. She looked at her home and moved toward the front porch. Joshua steadied her as they walked the final few yards to the steps. When they reached the spot of her attack, they both hesitated, each reliving for a split-second that awful night. Then arm in arm they climbed the steps and disappeared into the cabin.

❦ ❦ ❦

After getting her settled in bed, Joshua looked around to make sure all was clear. It was really just habit. He could sense trouble before ever seeing anything, but there was still a part of him that preferred a visual inspection of things.

When he was finished he went to Clarisse's room. She was conscious and smiled as he entered. It was good to see her smile once more, and he was thankful that the Lord had answered their prayers.

"Alone now, just you and me," she started. "I believe there are things that you need to explain. In my mind, I still see things that are beyond my comprehension. I dare say I'm not sure what was real and what was imagined."

"My Clarisse, you have been through a traumatic ordeal. It would only be natural if your mind were a bit bewildered."

"Do not patronize me! I *will* know what happened and who you really are! Joshua, you have hidden secrets. It's time you share them with me."

He hesitated, and then responded, "You are correct that I conceal some things from you, but it's for your own safety."

"No, I do not accept that! It seems to me there was a hidden reason for my attack. I remember you coming to my rescue, but dressed differently. I remember flames and screams from my attackers! I remember the smell of burning flesh! John Collins cannot be found anywhere. You speak in riddles to me. If you care for me at all, it's now time that you share the truth with me!"

Joshua knew this time would come. He had played it over and over in his mind. How could he share with her the direction her life was to take?

How could he convince her that the forces of hell itself had been directed to kill her?

"You're right. I do care for you, more than you know. What is it you wish to know?"

Clarisse closed her eyes and took a deep breath. When she opened them she looked Joshua straight in the eyes. "Are you an angel?"

"No."

"Has someone sent you here to protect me?"

"Yes."

"Who would that be?"

Joshua studied her face. A million questions were there. How was he to answer? He looked into her eyes and allowed her to see a quick glimpse of the Creator's heavenly realm. Although it was just an instant, Clarisse caught her breath at the magnificence she saw.

"Joshua, you say you are no angel. What I see is truly a vision of heaven itself!"

"Clarisse let me share with you what I can. It will be hard to accept, but I ask that you trust what I say."

Clarisse looked at him in wonder. She didn't know what she was about to hear, but she felt in her heart that this was a man whom she could trust. He had saved her life. There had to be a reason, and she felt she was about to learn why.

"Clarisse, I'd wished that I could have kept these things from you a while longer, but it's proper now to allow you to know what lies ahead for you…and me. What other questions would you ask?"

"You didn't answer my first question. If you are not an angel, then what are you…a devil? No man can do the things I've seen you do."

Joshua took her hands in his and gave them a reassuring squeeze. "My dear Clarisse, I am no angel. I'm as mortal as you are. I am, however…different." As he looked into her dark brown eyes, he knew that she was experiencing the same thing he had experienced that night in Corsair's apartment. That night, yet to be, Corsair struggled as he did now to share heavenly concepts.

As Clarisse was drawn deeper, she realized there was a connection between Joshua and herself. It was stronger than any bond she'd known. "When I look into your eyes, I see things that cannot be. If you are in fact mortal, then where do you come from?"

"What is it you see?"

"I see things too wonderful to tell. It does appear to be heaven. What a marvelous place you come from!"

"Look closer, what else do you see?"

Moments went by in silence. A troubled look came over her face. "I see distress and troubles. I see things too awful to mention. What terrible creatures are these that attack you? Why are you dressed in strange clothing? The woman by your side; who is she? She resembles me, but that cannot be. I've never done these things. What does all this mean Joshua? How can such a wonderful place be so full of evil?"

Joshua pulled back a bit and broke the connection as he spoke. "Your vision is in part. That tiny bit of heaven you saw is real. The evil forces you saw…are real. There is an eternal struggle between good and evil—and we've become a part of it."

"No! I will have no part with evil! God's love is what I seek!"

"And God's love is what will sustain us. Clarisse, evil is a part of this world. We're also a part of this world, and we've been called upon to help the Creator in this battle. The attack on you was not random. The enemy seeks to destroy you."

"Me! Why would anyone seek to kill me? I'm but an insignificant waitress at an insignificant inn."

"That's what you believe to be true. In reality, you are more important than you think."

"How would you know these things? Can you see into the future?"

With that statement, Joshua at first hung his head. How should he answer? After a moment of thought, he again looked at Clarisse. She was waiting for his answer, but he could tell she was beginning to realize her life was changing even as they spoke. "I can't see your immediate future. I do know, however, what the far-flung future may hold for you. You must understand, Clarisse, that you and I are mortals who will, in the future, battle the forces of evil as the Creator wishes. I am what is known as a Kalatar. You will become one as well, if we succeed in rescuing you here in this time from the assassins sent to destroy you."

Clarisse was stunned, and then spoke. "I'm not a soldier! I battle no one! Your speech is almost blasphemous! God is sovereign. We worship Him while we are here, but He needs no man to fight His battles!"

"You say that you battle no one. I must ask you a question now. Was John Collins an evil man?"

Clarisse was stunned to have Collins' name brought into this conversation. "Yes, very evil."

"Did you not battle him? Clarisse, you fought with the heart of a warrior. You never gave up. When all was lost, you found the inner strength to launch one final attack of your own. I tell you a truth: John Collins was not acting on his own lustful intentions that night. His directive was to kill you while I was detained. His own evil desires caused your death to be delayed till he'd had his way with you. That delay gave me enough time to defeat those who wished to keep me from your side. You fought him that night mentally and physically. My regret is that you suffered at his hand. Death was too good for him."

"You killed those men that night. Does not the Holy Scriptures say we must not take the life of another?"

Joshua knew this question would come up, it always does. "Clarisse, we are at war. We—you and I—are given a mandate to seek and destroy the enemies of our Creator. At times these enemies are spiritual beings, and sometimes they are mortals controlled by evil forces. Collins and his conspirators were evil men controlled by evil forces. We will not weep for them. We mourn only the loss of those who partake of the same oath we have…to The Order of Kalatar."

Although a lot of information was being conveyed to her, Clarisse absorbed it all. "You speak of me as if you have known me in the past, yet that cannot be. I have accomplished none of these feats you mention. When in the past have I fought with you?"

"Clarisse, you have asked me where I come from. You must now try to understand a hard thing. The Creator has sent me to rescue you, here in this time and place. You see, I come from a future time. It's a time when you *will* battle the enemy by my side. It's a time in which you do wondrous things for the cause of righteousness. You, Clarisse…are a powerful force in my time. The enemy wants you destroyed, and he has gone to great lengths to find you here, in your time to end your life. I have come to save you and help you understand your future."

Clarisse rose from her bed and walked to the window and gazed out. Her mind, although struggling with some concepts, seemed to accept all that Joshua shared. It appeared she was the prize to be won in this battle. Her death brought victory to God's enemies, while her salvation, with Joshua's help, would bring life and future victories over evil.

She turned back towards Joshua as she spoke, "The images I saw when I gazed into your eyes—you have been to heaven?"

"Yes, many times. I reside there, as you will when the time comes. Before we talk of heaven, though, there is work here that needs to be finished first. There may be two more attempts on your life. We must be vigilant."

"How can I visit heaven without dying?"

"It's difficult to understand, but it is a truth."

Clarisse was calm, perhaps a little numb. "Who else is here that would wish to take my life? Collins was an evil man, and you could *feel* that there was something evil in him. I don't feel that with anyone else."

Joshua was in awe that Clarisse already seemed to sense these spiritual concepts. "The next attack may be from a demonic source. Collins was about to reveal the identity of a powerful man here in Salem that sent him. It may have been a man, or it may have been a spirit who has taken human form. We don't know yet. We'll do what we can to identify him or wait for him to reveal himself."

Clarisse walked back to where Joshua was seated. She sat next to him on a wooden bench and took his hand. "I feel comforted by your presence even though you talk of my death. I can sense the things you tell me are true. I do not feel adequate to the task, but with you by my side, I will try to follow your leading. You have shown great compassion towards me, and I feel a great bond growing between us."

And with that she allowed Joshua to draw close and embrace her. It was the first real contact he'd had with her since leaving his time period. It was so good to hold her again. As he looked into her eyes once more, he took a chance and tenderly kissed her. It wasn't a long, lingering kiss, but a simple one. She rested her head on his shoulder then fell asleep while in his arms. The attack had left her weakened, and this conversation had taken its toll on her.

Joshua carried her to her bed and laid her down. Gathering a large quilt from the end of the bed, he covered her and stepped back. How beautiful she looked, even though her innocence was lost, both spiritually and physically. She would undeniably awaken a different person. He now had an ally in this battle. Although she was weak physically, her spirit would be strengthened and a help to him in battle.

Joshua now took the time to kneel beside her bed. "Father, I ask this night that you strengthen Clarisse for the battles ahead. Help me, I pray, to make the proper decisions concerning her welfare. Give us both your grace as we battle your enemies. Amen." Joshua got up, walked to the corner of the room, sat down in a wooden rocker, and fell asleep.

CHAPTER 20

❁

The next morning, Joshua woke first. He brewed some coffee and started breakfast, which consisted of a few eggs, a little bacon, and a couple of biscuits from her clapboard. The smells soon woke Clarisse, and she wandered into the room where Joshua was. It was a combination kitchen and living area. He tried to be upbeat as he greeted her. "Good morning Clarisse. I hope you have slept well after our talk last night."

She rubbed the sleep from her eyes and slowly made her way to the kitchen table. "Yes, I did sleep well; better than I have in a long time. I seemed to sense your presence nearby. Was that a truth or a dream?"

"No, it was not a dream. You'll find that you will definitely know when I am near, or when I'm in danger. We'll become very close in spirit."

"Only in spirit? You seem to know more about me than I know about you."

Joshua was taken aback a little. "We'll become very close as time passes."

"Are we lovers…in the future of course?" she smiled a bit as she hesitated with the sentence.

Joshua wasn't prepared for this conversation. He poured her a cup of coffee and set a plate in front of her before he answered. "It's not as you might think. We will become very close," he repeated.

Clarisse thought best not to pursue this subject further. She bowed her head and blessed the food before her. She looked up at Joshua and seemed to have a twinkle in her eye; "I'll have more questions for you at a later time I'm sure." And with that, she tried to eat her breakfast, but found her appetite had waned.

Joshua set a small flask on the table in front of Clarisse. It was dark in color and had a strange top to it. "What is this?" she asked. "It's such a strange bottle. There is no cork as a stopper."

"It's something I brought with me on this journey. It will give you strength and help you to heal more quickly." He twisted off the cap and poured a tiny amount into a fresh cup. He handed it to Clarisse. "Now drink. You'll find its taste to be pleasant. This is called 'Salimar.'"

She took the cup in hand and, without a second thought downed it. She seemed more puzzled by the strange top on the bottle than the fact that she was drinking a healing balm from heaven itself.

Clarisse gained strength in the following days. Joshua took care of her and rationed the mysterious medicinal elixir poured from the bottle with the strange top. Her appetite was still not good, and she wasn't able to keep much down. They took daily short walks with the distance growing as her strength increased.

It was now nearing the end of May, and the wild flowers around the small cabin began to bloom. Their walks were getting closer to Salem Town, so Joshua thought it a good idea to go to the Holystone and see the Putmans. They had sent some food with young William Proctor, which helped. Joshua wanted to thank them and see what news was transpiring concerning the events of the day.

It seemed that walking hand in hand had become natural, but as they approached town they realized that any outward show of affection was to be discouraged. The Puritan ideals concerning courtship were foreign to Joshua, but he didn't want any attention drawn their way. As they approached Essex Street, the smell of the morning air around the harbor and the increased activity of the seagulls were refreshing to Clarisse. It seemed to rejuvenate her. As the traffic increased on their short journey, Joshua noticed that people wouldn't look them in the eye. Some turned and crossed the street rather than have to confront them with a morning greeting. Clarisse also grew quiet as she felt the chill in the social air.

The door of the Holystone swung open, and once more they heard the noise and the clatter of the inn's hospitality. Silas Putman saw them enter and ran to greet them with open arms. This warm greeting was encouraging, and smiles were soon back as Hannah made her way from the kitchen and gave Clarisse a big hug. They made their way to Joshua's favorite table, and soon it was full with hot bacon, eggs, and coffee. Fresh bread was just coming out of the ovens, and it eventually made its way to the table as well, along with newly churned butter and fruited jams.

"You look so wonderful!" Mrs. Putman would say as she made several trips back and forth. "It's just so good to see you. We've missed you greatly. Many of our patrons have asked about you."

After chatting for a short time with Abigail, Clarisse said to the men, "I believe I'll go check on things in the kitchen. It would be good for me to talk with Hannah for a while. I don't seem to have much appetite this morning," and she scurried off.

Joshua looked at Silas and asked, "You say people have asked about Clarisse. What is it they have asked? Is it about her welfare, or is it gossip about the things concerning the day of the attack? Most people in this town barely know Clarisse."

Silas knew where Joshua was heading with the questions. "Most are concerned about her health. We know she was beaten badly. There are some though who are genuinely interested in the mystery of what happened for the safety of others in the town. No one seems to know what *really* happened that night. The doctor has seen fit, and rightly so, to keep things concerning his patients confidential. So that in itself breeds inquisition. There are some that no matter what happens in the town seem hell-bent on taking a small morsel of information and making something of it. As they spread their rumors, the mystery grows."

"And what are some of the rumors?"

"Well, some folks believe, as we do, that Clarisse was attacked by John Collins and his two friends. They are nowhere to be found—which adds to that theory. Some believe you had a hand in the mystery."

"People believe that I could have had a part in harming Clarisse?"

"No. Some believe you killed those three for their attack on Clarisse."

"What proof might they have?"

"Rumors…just rumors, my friend. To quite a few people you appear to be quite a mysterious person yourself."

"Are there other 'rumors'?"

With that, Silas paused and looked around the room. When he spoke, it was in hushed tones. "These are dark times, Joshua. There are many accusations here and in Salem Village that are causing a lot of innocent people pause for concern. The Reverend Parris…he seems to believe it's his God-given duty to root out every person associated with witchcraft in our communities. People are scared. Scared of the unknown, and scared also of people they have known for years."

"Am I or Clarisse being accused?"

"No, but there's not much known about you, and Clarisse has always been considered by some as an outsider. Some folks believe you two may be living in sin out near the swamp. There is also the story of a strange hooded man who brought Clarisse to the doctor. His wife stated that the man was quite a large, shadowy character. It seemed as if his image was hidden from her and the doctor even though he was standing right before them. He even paid them more than necessary for her care. That is what feeds some rumors. Were you that man, my friend?"

"Silas, you're right when you say these are dark times. I hope you'll trust me when I say that Clarisse and I have nothing to stand accused of. We're mysterious to some—that is true. But the evil that lurks around the street corners of Salem Town is something we wish to overcome just as much as the Reverend Parris. It's an evil that should be feared more than a perceived sin I may be committing."

"Then we'll speak no more of this. No matter what happens, you are always welcome here."

Abigail stepped from the kitchen and came over to the table. "Clarisse is taken ill! She's out back in the privie. Mrs. Putman is with her. She believes Clarisse should visit the doctor again."

Joshua rushed outside and met the women as they returned from the privie. Clarisse was pale and was helped along by Mrs. Putman. "What little breakfast she had didn't agree with her, I'm afraid."

"Clarisse, we should get you back to your cabin," Joshua started.

Mrs. Putman was emphatic. "No! She needs to see the doctor! If you'll not take her, then I will!"

Joshua was taken back by Mrs. Putman's forcefulness. "You're right. We'll go there immediately." He thanked Silas for his hospitality and his friendship, and they left.

Joshua gave Clarisse an arm to lean on as they made their way through the streets leading to the doctor's house. "What seems to be wrong Clarisse? You seemed to be coming along. The Salimar I've given you should help you grow stronger and heal you from the inside out."

"I just feel ill, that is all. It's hard to explain. I do feel stronger in many ways, but my stomach doesn't want to accept nourishment."

Up the steps to the front porch they walked, and with each step Joshua recounted the events of the fateful night of their first visit. Had he missed something? Was there some attack on her that he had missed? The door opened, and they were ushered into the home of Dr. Browne. After the doctor greeted them, he took Clarisse into his office to check her condition. Joshua was left to worry even though it did no good. Whether in the 21st century or here in the 17th, doctor visits were still the same. The concerned party was left to sit and wait. "At least in my era there are old magazines to look at," he joked with himself. Time seemed to drag by, and finally Joshua was summoned into the office with Clarisse and the doctor.

The doctor seemed grave and disturbed a bit. "I understand you're a good friend of this young woman. She wants me to include you in our conversation that concerns her health. She seems to be recovering quite rapidly from her recent attack. I'm amazed at that. I've never seen injuries heal so quickly."

"Then what is the cause of this illness she suffers from at this time?" Joshua asked.

"This *illness*, as you state, is quite easy to diagnose. Your friend Clarisse is with child."

"What!? That's not possible!" Joshua's voice rose as he spoke. "This can't be!" He looked at Clarisse who only hung her head. He felt ashamed that he had allowed such an outburst. He quickly calmed himself. *This isn't good.*

The doctor continued. "It is *indeed* possible. Whether from her recent attack or her association with you, she is quite pregnant. It's not my place to judge, but there are stories of the two of you living under the same roof. It would be quite natural to think that this could happen."

"I assure you, doctor, that our relationship has been completely platonic. I've only cared for Clarisse and helped her as she has healed. She has no one else to help her."

"Then it's from the attack. Rape further complicates this matter."

"Why would that be so?" questioned Joshua.

"I see you are truly new to our town. You must understand the thinking of some of these townsfolk. If this were an illegitimate child from a sinful relationship, the church could address that issue and forgiveness could be extended. A child born from a rape is different. It could be thought of as a union with the devil. Men are reluctant to admit that they have evil desires toward women and will be quick to find a scapegoat, sometimes that being the devil. Add to this situation the fact that no man was found who attacked Clarisse. It would be easy for some to consider her conception as a joining with Satan himself."

Joshua moved to Clarisse's side. Tears were now running down her cheeks, and he wiped them away with the back of his hand. Joshua looked at the doctor and said, "I've been told that you honor the privacy of your patients. We appreciate that. This matter must remain quiet for now. Further rumors would not be a good thing at this time for Clarisse or this town."

"Sir, my confidentiality is a sure thing. However, people will talk. There are those who know already that Clarisse was taken ill and brought here. Speculation will fuel more rumors. I'll be available for you and Clarisse with whatever you need."

Joshua thanked the doctor, paid him, and the two of them left. Clarisse seemed over her nausea for now. *Morning sickness. This complicates things. I never knew she had once carried a child.* "Lord help me," he silently prayed.

They walked a ways in silence till Clarisse opened up. "Do you think less of me now?"

Joshua was shocked. "Why would I think less of you? You had no control over what happened that night."

"It's something I should have prevented. I should have fought harder. I should have allowed him to kill me rather than give in to him!"

They were just turning up the narrow pathway leading to her home when Joshua stopped and turned toward her. He took her hand in his and matched his eyes with hers. "My dear Clarisse, I love you. I could never think ill of you."

It was done. Finally, he declared to her what he had wanted to since he first saw her in this era. Once again tears welled up in her eyes and spilled over and down her cheeks. This time though, tears of joy. "Oh Joshua, I've long wished to hear those words. I was afraid I never would. My heart is full this day!"

He took her in his arms and held her tight. He wanted this moment to last forever. He knew it wouldn't. The joy of this moment was still overshadowed by the dilemma they found themselves in. This pregnancy was something he could not have anticipated for sure. How would this affect the near future events? The enemy would use this to its advantage. There were still more attempts to be made on her life. How would her strength hold up with the added strain of an unborn child within her? How would the townsfolk react when it became common knowledge of her condition? So many questions, but there he stood with the love of his life in his arms. He held her even tighter, reluctant to let go.

❦   ❦   ❦

During the next few days, Joshua took the opportunity to teach Clarisse more about what he was sent to do and how important it was that she survive.

"You tell me that you travel directly from here to heaven regularly. Can you show me?" she questioned.

Joshua thought how easy it would be to take her and whisk her away to his heavenly sanctuary. "I can't take you there at this time. If we don't defeat the powerful enemies that have traveled back to this time, we can't imagine what havoc they would wreck here unchecked. I'd find a different world awaiting me when I return to my time."

"Then you plan to leave me?" She looked startled at the thought of his leaving.

"It will be for a time. If we achieve victory here we'll meet again someday and you'll be the teacher and I the pupil."

This didn't please her one bit. "And what if we don't succeed? What if the enemy is too strong?"

"If the enemy wins—if we die here together—then we'll see each other in heaven as martyred saints. Any child of God who accepts the sacrifice that Jesus made for us will have that same eternal life."

"Then I pray the time will be long before we engage these enemies you speak of." Clarisse looked more saddened as she seemed to think of more complicated questions. "We won't be as husband and wife there though. True?"

The mention of marriage surprised Joshua. "That's true, but we'll have a more fulfilling relationship. Trust me. I've seen our future and it's full without a doubt."

Clarisse rubbed her hands over her stomach. Although she was pregnant she hadn't begun to show any outward signs of carrying a child. "What of this unborn child…does he not need a father as well as a mother?"

Joshua fumbled for words. Marriage was still the theme of her query. "I'm truly sorry, but I have no knowledge of this child. In our future, you were reluctant to share your past with me. I was just so happy to share with you the things we had in common that your past was never discussed much. I always believed that you held secrets in your past that were dark. I believe now that you wanted to shield me from the hurt you must have suffered in the past."

With that, Joshua steered their conversation away from the uncertainly of their near future and concentrated more on the here and now. He explained to her how the cascading waterfall of colors was his portal to heaven—that in time she would make her first journey through it. He taught her that he could transverse the natural and spiritual realms in the blink of an eye. He tried to tell her what their heavenly compound was like and about the sights and sounds of heaven.

He showed her his battle gear, complete with his bladed, flaming sword. With just a simple thought it would burst into flames. She showed both awe and fear at this sight. Joshua retracted the flames and it became a short steel blade once again. He handed it to her and she marveled at the intricate, jeweled carving on the handle. "That's the emblem that designates that the owner is of The Order of Kalatar," he continued. "Most enemies fear even the sight of it for they know their end is near."

Clarisse turned it over and over in her hands. Although rugged, it was light in her hand. The blade was razor-sharp. "Has this weapon destroyed many?"

"Yes, it has. Mostly they have been spiritual enemies, but there have also been some mortals who were controlled by Satan, like Collins."

At the mention of his name, Clarisse looked disturbed, and as she gazed at the shiny metal blade, it appeared to glow a bit. "Try to concentrate on the fiery flame you saw earlier, Clarisse," he encouraged. "It may be that you already possess the ability to use it." She gazed as one looking into a crystal ball, but the blade only glowed as she held it up. After a time she gave up and handed it back to Joshua.

"It's undeniably an awesome weapon. I can feel that as I hold it. It's hard to believe that I'll possess one like it in the future."

"You will, Clarisse. You'll win many great victories for our cause."

"Now, that's a hard thing to believe," she finally smiled. "I don't feel like a warrior right now." She pointed once more to her waistline and made an expanding motion with her hands.

CHAPTER 21

Warmer weather arrived, and with it Clarisse grew stronger. Her morning sickness had passed, and their afternoon walks were a tonic for her as they enjoyed the wildflowers and the sunshine. As they returned to the cabin one late afternoon, the area near her cabin began to shimmer and shine with a multitude of colors from the treetops to the ground. A loud deafening roar began, and Clarisse clung to Joshua at the fearful yet awesome sight.

"Clarisse, we may have a visitor coming for dinner." Clarisse couldn't move an inch. "Come," he continued, "Let's greet our guest."

With that, they watched as a form slowly materialized in the mist and casually walked through the falling colors until he stood before them. He was dressed in battle garb much like Joshua except for a few differences, but the ever-present sword of The Order hung on his side. He seemed to be in awe himself as he saw Joshua and nodded his head in reverence as he addressed them. "I believe I'm at your service. My name is Nathaniel. We must talk. There's much to share."

The three comrades quickly entered the small cabin, and Clarisse set to making some coffee. Her hands trembled as she prepared the water. All the things Joshua had shared seemed as a dream to her. But now she had seen with her own eyes a visitor from heaven itself step through this gateway and into her home. The reality of her situation was finally setting in. She was in the midst of a struggle between good and evil, and she was the prize to be won or lost.

Joshua felt a bit odd as this newcomer looked him up and down. It seemed as if he couldn't take his eyes off of Joshua. "Forgive me for seeming in awe, but I never thought I'd find that which was described in my briefing. We knew there were disturbances that seemed to involve a member of The Order, but to believe one had traveled from the future seemed unbelievable. We could sense activity here, and I was sent to investigate and be of any help you might need. I pledge my life to your cause."

Joshua realized that like him, this member knew this mission was not only of great importance, but also that he might be called upon to give his life if necessary for victory to be achieved. "We appreciate your help, and while we share a cup of coffee, I'll fill you in on the situation."

With that, Joshua started from the beginning and explained what had happened in the future and why he was sent back to save Clarisse Corsairée. It reinforced to Clarisse the gravity of her situation. These were two men who would gladly give their lives to save her. She didn't feel she was as important as they suggested, but here they were, sitting in her kitchen, discussing what to do next. Their talks involved forming a plan to thwart the enemy.

She re-filled their cups a second and a third time but listened to every word. After Joshua finished his story, it was his turn to ask some questions of their new friend. "Tell me, Nathaniel, why were you the only one sent? In my time period, we would have sent a unit of six Kalatar."

"Six!" he responded. "What a blessing that would be! No, my friend, we don't have those numbers in our ranks in this era. I know the times are changing, but we've not needed great numbers to defeat those we face in the here and now. On rare occasions we might travel with one other, but usually we move about as single combatants. We do quite well, however. The enemy's agents in this time don't match up well with us. I realize my skills may not be as great as yours, but I hope they will tip the scales in your favor."

Joshua was glad to have help of any kind. "To have a comrade is, in fact, a great blessing. It'll take some pressure off of me as we decide, together, the best course of action." Nathaniel seemed pleased that Joshua was treating him as an equal.

It was decided that Nathaniel would scout about in the spiritual realm to see if he might gain any information on enemy activity. When needed, he could help guard Clarisse if, or when, Joshua might need to leave her for any amount of time. Their constant contact with each other would prove invaluable in defense of their position.

Things were shaping up, but Joshua was concerned about the unknown. Unknown were the plans of the enemy, the position of power they held in Salem Town, and what their next move was. Joshua much preferred to operate from an offensive posture. He would rather keep the enemy guessing what *his* next move was rather than trying to play defense. This was the ultimate chess game with the future to be won or lost.

Clarisse prepared a dinner of roast beef, roasted potatoes, and greens while the talks grew to a close. After the blessing over the meal, all three enjoyed a great time of fellowship. Clarisse was surprised that the situation she found herself in was feeling more natural. The talk had drifted from battle plans to discussing their own personal situations and how they were introduced into the heavenly ranks of The Order.

Nathaniel was a veteran of a number of battles against hell's forces. He was from England and became a career soldier who fought in the service of King Charles II. He was wounded in the Battle of Marston Moor in 1644. In a field hospital he found himself near death when an angel (or so he thought) appeared to him and explained how he was needed to fight a different foe than the one he had faced that day.

He thought he was delirious and dismissed the "angel" with the wave of his hand. But the images and the visions continued as he recovered from his wounds. As time passed, he discovered (as most do) it was his destiny to join the forces of the Creator who fight for truth and righteousness.

When it was Joshua's turn to share his story, he hesitated. "I'm afraid that what I reveal could have implications on Clarisse's future."

"And why would that be?" Clarisse responded as she actively joined the conversation.

"Things I reveal here today might shape the decisions you must make in the future."

Clarisse looked at Joshua with a slight smile. She was learning quickly about taking advantage of a situation. "You say that whatever knowledge I have about the future might affect the future itself. What if I die in this time period? There would then be no future for me. If I had *some* knowledge of your future, how do you know that the knowledge I take with me from this day forward wouldn't help shape your future?"

Joshua was impressed with her logic. "I'll admit that there are occasions I think of our time together in the future and wonder how you knew things about me that weren't generally known. It could be that this day was ordained to be. Perhaps, for the sake of our discussion, it might be wise to share what I feel lead to with both of you."

With that, he opened his heart and began to share his story. Nathaniel was eager to hear not only a story about the future but also how these two would learn and grow together as a fighting team.

It was in the late 20th century when Joshua met an attractive co-worker known as Corsair. He worked as a salesman and, not having any family to speak of, was quite a loner. Over a period of time their friendship grew.

Joshua was attracted to her but suppressed his feelings out of a sense of inadequacy. He didn't think her feelings would be mutual. After some time, strange things began to take place involving Corsair. They were things that appeared to be supernatural in nature. She was quite mysterious which attracted Joshua even more.

Corsair orchestrated events to draw the two of them closer together which, in turn, allowed her to eventually explain the Creator's plan for Joshua's life.

As Joshua shared his story, Clarisse seemed captivated. She hung on every word as she listened in fascination to a story about herself that would take place over 400 years in the future.

Joshua went on to explain his first experiences in heaven and how Corsair was there, by his side, ready and willing to enlighten him about his new surroundings.

Clarisse waited for a break in the story and interjected, "'Corsair.' You call me by that name in the future? That isn't my given name. In the future, do people choose to shorten their names?"

"There were many secrets about yourself you chose not to reveal to me. I found it easier to enjoy your presence and avoid too many questions."

"Are we lovers? In the future, I mean," she blushed at how the words sounded as they escaped her lips.

Joshua smiled. "Lovers, yes. But not as you might think. It's difficult to explain right now." Now it was his turn to blush a little. He looked at Nathaniel and thought it better to share more intimate thoughts with Clarisse later. Nathaniel nodded in agreement.

It was now getting late, and Nathaniel decided to leave. He would take his position in the spiritual arena giving them one last opportunity to allow Clarisse a glimpse of their powers and abilities. With just a nod "good-bye," Nathaniel instantly vanished from their sight. Joshua explained to Clarisse that he was still with them, but in the unseen netherworld that existed all around them. He would be vigilant and ever-watching, ready to pounce on any enemy that came his way.

CHAPTER 22

The month of May finally came to a close and with it the death of Sarah Osborne. She died in prison awaiting trial. Sarah had been one of the original three accused of witchcraft. The number of people arrested doubled during May, and the number now totaled over 60.

June started with the new Governor of Massachusetts, Sir William Phips, authorizing the courts to open and begin hearing the cases against the accused. This new court promptly tried Bridget Bishop, convicted her of witchcraft, and sentenced her to death.

June also brought a share of trouble for Clarisse and Joshua. Residents of Salem were expected to attend church services twice weekly. With her extended time of recovery from the rape and beatings, she hadn't been to church in quite a while.

It was only a matter of time before this was brought to the attention of the leaders of the church. Silas Putman paid a visit one bright sunny day and wasted no time about the purpose of his visit.

"I wanted to warn the two of you that there's talk in town about you. Folks understand you have been sick, but their patience is wearing thin. There are those who believe you should be attending services."

Joshua almost broke into laughter. "Surely the church has no say about the regularity of her church attendance!"

"Don't laugh my friend. The Church and the State are one. The leaders of the church dictate the laws we live by. There are powerful people in charge. You'll do well to watch how you conduct yourself around these people. Since it appears you're not familiar with the laws here, church attendance *is* mandatory." He apologized for being the bearer of bad news and reaffirmed his friendship with both of them. "I just don't want to see anything bad happen to you folks." And with that, he bid them "good day" and left.

Joshua turned and looked at Clarisse. She looked a bit sad and hung her head a little as he addressed her. "Why so sad? Is it such a bad thing to go to church?"

"You don't know the people there. These Puritans have strict beliefs that I've always found strange. They talk of God's love, but then make accusations that cause old women and little girls to be arrested. I fear Bridget Bishop won't be the last to be sentenced. They have always considered me an outsider. I fear we won't find a tender ear to hear our story once inside the doors of the church."

"We have nothing to be ashamed of," he responded but quickly realized once more that this was not his era. Things would be looked at differently.

"Joshua, you really don't understand. Even though my pregnancy may still be a secret, our living here in the woods is not. That alone will cause me great distress when I return to church. We are not husband and wife. Once word of me being with child is general knowledge, there will be no stopping the accusations, and the leaders will have reason to accuse me of anything that they like."

"Then what must we do?" The question was genuine, but Joshua was forming a plan he hesitated to mention.

Clarisse was still downcast. "I see no way out of this. I will be punished for my indiscretions, and later, who knows how these 'leaders' will interpret my physical situation."

"Let's take a walk," Joshua suggested. He took her by the hand and led her outdoors into the afternoon sunshine. They walked a ways and came to a large oak tree near the main road. They stopped and sat down near the base of it.

Joshua tenderly held her hand in his and looked into her eyes as he spoke. "Would the church look differently at our situation if we were married?"

Clarisse couldn't believe her ears. "Joshua!"

"Clarisse Corsairée, will you marry me?"

The words seemed to echo in her mind. *Marriage? No, it cannot be!* Surely she had heard wrong. "Joshua, you know not what you suggest!"

"But I do know. I've loved you from the first time my eyes met yours. Though it has spanned 400 years, my love for you has only grown stronger. That which was not permitted for me in the future may be our salvation here in the past. Do you love me as well? Once again I ask…will you marry me?"

Tears welled up in her eyes and spilled over and down her cheeks. The downcast look was gone and it was replaced with a wide smile. She giggled as she hugged his neck and said, "Oh Joshua, yes, I do love you…and yes, I will marry you!"

❦   ❦   ❦

Now there was much to do. If they were to attend church on Sunday, they would have to work fast. Joshua summoned Nathaniel and told him of their plan. He would stay with Clarisse while Joshua made his way to town to make the proper arrangements. His first stop was to the Holystone. He quickly cornered Silas and told him the good news. Silas grabbed him by the shoulders and shook him with congratulations. "If you can arrange things with the minister of Salem's church, we'll have a celebration dinner in your honor here Saturday afternoon!"

His next stop was to the church. Salem Town had had a succession of ministers who never stayed very long. Once they discovered the power struggles within the church, they left after a short time; or if they stayed, it was a sure thing that they would ruffle feathers and be asked to leave.

Reverend Trask was fairly new to Salem Town and met with Joshua to discuss the wedding. "With all this talk of witches and arrests, it would be a grand thing to have a wedding to celebrate. I know Saturday is short notice, but my wife and I would be honored to see you and your bride start a new life together."

Joshua thanked him and left. *Start a new life together. He doesn't know how true his words are.*

He hurried down one street and up another. Joshua knew the town well now. His last stop would be with the town silversmith. Edward Flint was the only one in town. He had a reputation of fairness, and the quality of his work was next to none. Many ships left Salem Harbor with his handcrafted jewelry on board.

Joshua picked out a plain silver band and paid Mr. Flint with gold coins taken from a small leather pouch. John Collins was still paying in more ways than one for his crimes. *Poetic.* Joshua mulled things over in his mind as he left the shop and headed home. *Home, it truly will be home for us, as least for a while.*

❦   ❦   ❦

Saturday came quickly. Clarisse couldn't sleep and she was up before dawn preparing a breakfast for her fiancé. Joshua met with Nathaniel who agreed to oversee the event so nothing might go wrong.

The Putmans and Martins were invited to attend the wedding, with dinner provided at the Holystone where the regulars would help celebrate at a small reception. All in all things were shaping up nicely.

Eleven o'clock arrived, and with it a carriage that Joshua had arranged. Clarisse emerged from the cabin dressed neatly in her Sunday best clothes. Although simple in style, Joshua thought she looked like an angel—his angel. They held hands all the way to town with little conversation. They both seemed full of joy in anticipation of what this day would bring.

The church was small by 21st century standards, but it seemed a long walk from the back of the church to the altar area where the Reverend stood waiting. Whether right or wrong, Joshua was going through with this. He never thought in his wildest dreams that he would ever be married, least of all in the 17th century.

The service was simple. The vows were heartfelt, and the silver ring glistened as the nervous groom placed it on her finger.

The ring was no sooner on Clarisse's finger than Joshua *felt* something amiss. Evil could be felt in the air, and he quickly caught himself just in time to respond to the question posed to him by the Reverend Trask.

"Do you promise to love this woman Clarisse? Will you love her in sickness and health, in riches and in want? Will you forsake all others and love her until death parts the two of you?"

Joshua looked her in the eyes and responded, "I will, of course."

Turning to Clarisse, the Reverend addressed her likewise: "Do you promise to love this man Joshua? Will you love him in sickness and health, in riches and in want? Will you forsake all others and love him until death parts the two of you?"

It was hard for her to speak. This man had come into her life, and the changes had happened so quickly. He had already rescued her from the jaws of death. He had nursed her back to health. She felt that she owed him more than she could ever repay. But he wasn't asking for repayment. He was asking her to join him in an everlasting covenant.

She firmly squeezed his hands and smiled as she said, "I will, Reverend. I will."

As the two looked into each other's eyes, it seemed as if they received a vision that showed all of heaven rejoicing. The scene was magnificent, and they barely heard Reverend Trask as he said, "Please kiss your bride."

The carriage awaited, and as they left the church, Joshua could see a man on a horse near the edge of the church property. *Holy ground. He can't come near.* The carriage quickly whisked them off once more, this time to the Holystone. As they made their way through the streets of Salem Town, it served notice to those who like to tell tales that Clarisse Corsairée would not be shamed tomorrow at church. Joshua had truly made an "honest woman" of her.

It was a festive atmosphere that greeted them as they entered the front doors of the inn. Cheers went up and hugs were the order of the day. Their private table was moved from the edge of the room to the middle, with other tables surrounding it. Food began to pour from the kitchen, and Clarisse marveled that she was the person being served by those she had waited on so often.

Joshua enjoyed the moment with his new bride but was ever vigilant. The last thing they needed was an attack from the enemy. As he allowed himself to indulge in the celebration, he found that people were genuinely happy for him and Clarisse. *What would they say if they all knew the truth about us?*

Evening came all too quickly, and soon it was time to leave their friends and head home. All those who were married joked a little (even for Puritans) as they made their way out the door as husband and wife.

Dusk was drawing near as they stepped onto the porch of their cabin. "There's a tradition in our time for new couples starting out in life together," Joshua began.

"What might that be?"

"The groom carries the bride over the threshold, signifying his strength and conviction to care for his new bride."

"It sounds a bit odd to me, but if you must…."

With that, Joshua lifted her from the ground and gently carried her though the doorway and continued on into their bedroom. He didn't stop until he stood next to their bed. "It's here that I'll release you," he said as he laid her onto the bed.

He expected nature to take its course from there and waited for his bride to open her arms, inviting him to join her. Instead, he saw once more a fear creep over her. She began to cry…softly at first, as if she were ashamed of something; then harder until she was sobbing uncontrollably.

"My dear Clarisse, what is wrong?"

"I cannot do this! I love you more than you can know, but the thought of this is too painful! *His* touch is still a loathsome thing, and my mind will not release that memory. I am sorry. I feel I have already failed you as a wife!"

Joshua was stunned. No man can understand the pain a woman suffers from an attack such as this. *How long, Lord? How long must she suffer?* As she continued to cry, he gently eased himself onto the edge of the bed and tenderly stroked her hair to see if she would recoil from his touch. He could feel her take a deep breath, and as she exhaled relaxed a little.

"There is no need for more words, my love," he whispered. "You have in no way failed me. It is I who should have been more aware of what you have been through. For now, it is sufficient for me to be here and to hold you close."

Clarisse felt an easing of the anxiety and was comforted that Joshua was near. His gentle touch required no response from her, and she remembered a scripture that said, "love is not demanding, but patient and kind." She fell asleep to the sound of his whispered prayers in her ear…prayers for her complete healing.

CHAPTER 23

❀

Sunday morning, June 5th, came, and the sun shone through their bedroom window. It warmed their bodies as they lay together. Joshua stirred and remembered the time he woke up in Corsair's apartment. He found himself on a couch while she slept in her bedroom. Now he woke up to find her at his side.

The events of the night before seemed like a bad dream to him. He stroked Clarisse's hair once more as she turned toward him. She smiled and opened her eyes. Joshua held his breath—he silently prayed that she would be feeling better this morning.

She drew him close and tenderly kissed him. "My darling angel," she whispered. "I am sorry that my fears overtook me last night."

Joshua started to speak, but she placed a finger to his lips. "I fell asleep listening to your prayers for me. What a blessing you are, my dear Joshua. God is truly good to have allowed you to make my life complete. You are my protector, my best friend, the love of my life."

She drew even closer to him. No words were now spoken as husband and wife became one.

Joshua and Clarisse now shared a bond only a married couple can know. What John Collins tried to pervert was now the most beautiful thing these two mortals could share.

Time would tell if their decision to marry was correct. For now, nothing mattered except the fact that they were together as they felt they should always be…as husband and wife.

🍁   🍁   🍁

They weren't sure what to expect upon arriving for church. The closer they came to the church the thicker the crowd was. Some people made their way without looking about much. Church was a solemn affair and not to be taken lightly.

Others fixed their eyes on Clarisse and watched her as she made her way into the church and into the designated seating areas for men and women. It wasn't hard to tell what could be on their minds. Joshua seated himself near the back of the church along with other men of the town. Just as the day before, he sensed an evil presence nearby.

Reverend Trask took his place behind the lectern and cleared his throat as he address the congregation: "My dear folks, it is always a pleasure to come to you with good news. Yesterday in this very sanctuary, I had the privilege of uniting in holy matrimony two people from Salem Town. The former Clarisse Corsairée and Joshua Lunt are now husband and wife."

"No!" came a scream from the far side of the sanctuary.

Reverend Trask was startled at the outburst.

"Do they think a marriage will make her respectable?" from another part of the building.

"I hear she is with child!" added a third.

"Leave her be!" yelled Silas Putman. "She is a fine woman to be sure!"

"If that be true, then why does the constable wait near the road for her this day? There are accusations against her!"

With that, Joshua looked at a frightened Clarisse and then turned his attention to the open doorway leading out onto the front lawn of the church property. There amongst a grove of trees stood a shadowy figure. *The constable. It's not a wonder why he lingers there. He can't approach us while we stand on holy ground. At least we now know who our second adversary will be.*

Reverend Trask pleaded with the congregation. "People, please! This is uncalled for! The Lord would not have us act this way in His house!"

Joshua rose and quickly stepped to Clarisse. He grabbed her by the hand, and together they hurriedly exited the building. Others followed behind. Silas was at their heels and waved off those who continued to hurl insults as they left.

Outside the air was thick with a putrid smell of sulfur. Joshua was surprised that Clarisse was aware of it as well. The other mortals in the area sensed nothing out of the ordinary. Silas held back as his two friends headed for the road and the constable who waited there. The people exiting the church held back near the steps of the building.

Clarisse pulled on Joshua's arm. "We mustn't go on! He waits for us, Joshua!"

Joshua continued to pull her along until they came to within a few feet of the road. "What is it you want?" he asked in a whisper so only the constable and his wife could hear.

"You know all too well what I seek," he hissed. "Only the death of this 'witch' will quench my thirst this day. Step into the road and we'll settle the matter without delay."

With that he mounted his horse and announced for all to hear, "Clarisse Corsairée, you are hereby accused this day of witchcraft! You will surrender yourself at once to be taken into custody! And you, Joshua Lunt, if that is truly your name, are under arrest for the murder of John Collins and his two shipmates! You will also surrender now!"

The two accused took a few steps back as the horse reared up on hind legs. The turf was pounded and dust rose as he returned his front hoofs to the ground. "Don't fear, Clarisse, he can't cross the road to arrest us. This is holy ground, and he fears it as much as he fears me."

"I need not approach you. Others will bring you to me." As he said this, they saw the crowd moving towards them. The use of the word "witch" was all that some needed to hear. While there were those who turned to run, others seemed all too eager to assist the constable.

"Witch! He called her 'witch'!"

"Stay away from her. She may cast a spell your way!"

"I knew there was something evil about her!"

Those gathered near these happenings didn't know and couldn't recall what happened next. A bolt of lightning came from nowhere and struck the earth at the feet of the constable's horse. It reared up and bucked the rider to the ground. Smoke and haze were everywhere, so none could see that the constable was under attack. A blazing sword flashed here and there as the constable struggled to regain his feet. An ordinary mortal would have been killed, but the constable was neither ordinary nor mortal. He fielded the blows as he tried to regain his footing.

"Nathaniel!" Joshua took the opportunity this distraction afforded him to gather Clarisse and head for Silas' carriage. The three ran as if their lives depended on it...for surely they did. Once in the carriage, Silas slapped the horse with the reins and raced down the road. As they looked back they could see people scattering from the church grounds. They ran in all directions as the smoke grew thicker.

With a loud clap of thunder, the demon who had disguised himself in human form disappeared with Nathaniel in pursuit. Joshua knew he would be no match for this demon, but was thankful for the time it would allow them to retreat and form a better plan.

As they raced through Salem Town Joshua could see that Silas was visibly shaken. He guided the carriage behind the Holystone and pulled the horse to a stop without a word. When he did speak, he seemed to have gathered himself.

"I don't know what happened back there...nor do I wish to know. I feel you two are good people who need now to leave with all haste. Folks will not stop until you are in custody."

"We have unfinished business here first, Silas. We can't leave just yet. There's a battle with evil for sure, and the life of Clarisse hangs in the balance."

"You must not stay! We will all stand accused with you if you linger!"

"Then we'll retreat to some desolate area for this confrontation. Are you aware of any such place?"

He paused a moment to think. "It may be possible. There is one place where no one goes. It's hard to get to, but it's a very private place."

"Then we shall make haste, for our adversary will not wait in pursuing us."

With that, Silas disappeared into the inn and returned in a few minutes with a burlap sack that he threw into the carriage. "Here are a few supplies that may be of use to you," he said, and then he turned horse and carriage around and headed down Becket Avenue toward the docks. The sound echoed against the buildings as they hurried along. Being Sunday, the streets were empty, and the lonely carriage quickly found its way to Salem Harbor.

Silas turned toward a place beyond where the shipping vessels docked. They slowed as they made their way eastward to where the water was too shallow for the big ships. It was an area where ferries delivered goods from one side of the bay to the other. Ferries large and small lined private docks where business on a smaller scale was conducted each day.

Silas pulled to a stop near one dock that had a small rowboat tied up. "I have a relative who owns this dock and boat. If you take it, you'll find it but a short trip out there, to Jeggle's Island." He pointed to the middle of the harbor. A tiny island stood out against the skyline. Even though it appeared small, there were plenty of trees blocking the view of the island's interior.

"It has no value and is quite desolate. No one goes there. You may be safe for a while I pray."

"It will suit our needs very well," Joshua responded. "I'm sorry that you have become involved in this matter. We'll pray you suffer in no way but that the Lord will bless you for your help this day." Silas smiled and nodded as they stepped down from his carriage. A quick flick of his wrist brought the reins to bear on the backside of his horse as he turned and quickly headed back toward town.

Joshua turned to Clarisse. "I'm sorry you must go through this, but it's you he's after and we must battle him on our terms. He won't surprise us now that we know the form he's taken. However, we may not see him again as the constable, but as he really is."

"And what is he in truth?" she asked.

"This creature is one of the three demons from the future. The first one we defeated was deceptive and crafty. It was the same type of spirit that tempted Eve in the garden. Just as the serpent enticed Eve to disobey the Creator, I was, in the same way, also enticed. This devil tempted me to engage in combat with it. In doing this, I forgot my first duty: to protect you. I succumbed to his tempting just as Adam and Eve did.

"This second one will be more of a warrior, I believe. He seemed confident and had no fear when he confronted us earlier. The Holy Scriptures tell of our eternal enemy Satan going about as a roaring lion seeking to devour all he encounters. I believe we'll need a place like this, away from people, to engage this 'roaring lion.'"

"And the third...what manner of evil will it show itself to be?" she asked.

"We must concentrate on this adversary first. Then we'll move on to our next obstacle."

As the sound of the horse's hoofs faded in the distance, the two lonely figures wasted no time in transferring the sack of supplies to the small boat. Joshua jumped from the dock to the boat and then held out his hands for Clarisse to join him. She seemed unsteady as she climbed into the boat and quickly sat down holding onto the rearward seat as if she might be rocked overboard.

After untying the ropes that held the craft to the dock, he pushed off and pointed the bow toward the ominous-looking isle. The sun was hot and bore down on him as he rowed in quiet desperation. This would not be a good spot to be if their adversary decided to reappear.

Clarisse remained mute, sitting stiff in her seat facing Joshua. It was apparent that the movement of the craft beneath her didn't sit well. Her face was white as wool, and the perspiration beaded on her forehead. She remained still as if trying to hold back the urge to heave overboard.

On out through Palfrey's Cove, and after what seemed an eternity, they neared the rocky shore of Jeggle's Island. Joshua found a small inlet where the water was quite calm, and the rocks parted enough to allow him to guide their craft to a stop. He jumped from the boat into about three feet of water and pulled it up to the gravely shore.

Once again on dry ground, he helped Clarisse from their tiny vessel. It proved to be no small task. Shaky and weak in the knees, she immediately dropped to the ground and lost what little she had in her stomach. After all was expelled, she hid her face in her hands and started to cry, softly at first, and then harder until her sobs echoed from the surrounding rocks.

Joshua took her in his arms and rocked her back and forth, holding her ever so tightly. "My dear, I apologize. I didn't realize this short trip would overcome you so. It seems easy for me to forget your condition."

She pulled slightly away from him. "My condition? Joshua, what *is* 'my condition'? Why am I the prize to be won here in this barren place? I feel I am of no value to anyone! Look at me, covered in my own vomit! I'm not this great warrior princess you seek to rescue! I am but a shamed woman banished from my home and sought by the authorities—who will surely punish me for my grievous faults!"

Joshua, in his haste to save her, had in fact neglected her. He had forgotten how little she really understood about their situation. *How could I be so stupid?* He took a cloth from a pocket and wiped the sweat from her brow. He pulled out the small bottle without a cork and gave her a sip of Salimar.

"Forgive me. I know now how difficult this is for you. I don't understand why things have developed as they have, but I know that the Lord has a plan for you. I know you feel sick and confused right now, but you'll become strong and confident. You *will* be a force that the enemy will not want to deal with in the future. That is why it's important that we continue on. The future lies ahead…and it's a future where you must survive to battle on."

Clarisse caught her breath and buried her head into her husband's shoulder. She had thrown her arms around him and now held him tightly. No words were spoken, and time seemed to stand still. The tiny sip she had taken calmed her stomach, and soon she released her hold and pulled back.

"What now is our plan?"

Joshua could see a new resolve in her eyes. "We'll make for the interior, there beyond those trees, and wait. I believe the time will be short until we see the 'constable' again. When we do, he'll not be in the same form as before. He may be an awesome sight…but do not fear, the Lord is on our side."

They slowly got to their feet, and as Joshua threw the sack of provisions over his shoulder, they made their way up through the tree line and on toward the middle of the island.

As the two fugitives continued on through the now thinning trees, they could see the more desolate part of the island. It appeared to be as an ancient natural amphitheater might look—a clearing surrounded by the trees, void of any type of vegetation. As if cursed from ages past, nothing appeared to have grown. What stood before them were acres of arid ground.

One lone boulder lay in the middle of the natural arena, and one lonely figure leaned against it.

"Nathaniel! Clarisse, look…he's alive!" They both broke into a run to cover the remaining distance between them.

"Ah…my good friends, what took you so long to get here?" he joked. "I've risked life and limb to be here, and you two decide to take a leisurely jaunt in a pleasure craft in this afternoon's sunshine."

With that comment, Clarisse frowned, being reminded so quickly of her sickness in the harbor. Joshua pulled her close and nodded toward her so Nathaniel might see that he had made a verbal blunder. He quickly steered the conversation away from her.

"Tell us, what's become of the constable?"

"Yes, rightly so. I'm afraid I was no match for his speed. In the human form he took, I was able to catch him off-guard. Once we entered the spiritual realm, he transformed himself and quickly sped away. It was as if I was of no consequence to him at all."

"Let's hope that ignoring you may be the one mistake this creature will regret. What form did he revert to?"

"I've not seen one like it before. He was not large and lumbering, but sleek and fast. I wasn't able to engage him as he rapidly sped away. I knew there was no way to follow him even though I tried for a spell."

"Well, one thing is sure; he'll hunt us down before long. Who knows that he may be watching us at this very moment waiting to pounce? What will our plan be when the time arrives?"

"That, my friend, is what we must make haste to do: form a plan."

As it was getting late in the day, they gathered a bit of wood and built a little campfire, something to warm them a bit. The trees would shield the smoke and flame from any eyes off shore that might look their way. They talked a while of what they would do, but eventually they all grew silent. Now they were left to wait…wait for victory or defeat, wait for life or death. Time would tell which it would be.

CHAPTER 24

❦

Clouds began to roll in from the east. The sun scurried to the west as if it were being chased by the ominous shadows. A mist hung in the air—a prelude to the light rain to follow. Joshua and Nathaniel looked at each other and tried to keep from frightening Clarisse. They could both *feel* the pending storm and knew there would be more to deal with than the weather.

Clarisse would have none of their charades. "Something is about to happen. I can feel it. Am I correct?"

The two men looked at each other and silently acknowledged that Clarisse was in sync with them.

"You have become very perceptive," Joshua started. "Can you now begin to see why you're the prize in this deadly contest? Already you are beginning to feel the strength that lies within you. Your senses are in tune with what's happening. Usually these are things that must be taught to new members of our Order. You have a natural gift, and it shows us even more how valuable you are to the kingdom."

"Then what must I do?"

Nathaniel spoke up. "You will do nothing. Satan has a strategy for your destruction. It's our duty—and honor—to protect you even if it means we die trying."

The rain started, light at first, then it became more of a drizzle. It was just enough to make a body miserable. With no shelter in the center of the island, the three outcasts stood back to back and scanned the horizon for anything that moved.

A rumble of thunder rolled in, and with it a huge black cloud. It seemed to come from the east and circled the desolate area once, then hovered in place about 30 feet from them. The men drew their swords in anticipation of what the cloud might hold. They didn't have time to speculate. The huge cloud settled to the ground and was so dark it seemed to swallow the remaining light of day that surrounded them.

Suddenly, the cloud cracked open as one might crack an egg. It split in half, top to bottom, and out of it spilled a stench from the pits of hell itself. A greenish, black liquid substance formed a puddle on the ground. Then, with a thundering sound that shook the area around them, their enemy from the future disembarked with a leap and a bound, landing in the middle of the cesspool.

Although he wasn't huge, he stood about seven feet tall. He was humanoid in form, but his skin was a pale gray. His eyes were blood red and void of emotion. His head was bare, save a few mangy shards of hair. Scars covered his bare arms, and he wore what appeared to be leather body armor covered with sharp metal studs. A soft devilish glow surrounded the creature.

In one hand he carried a halberd.[1] A broadsword hung from his waist, and his body was draped with a long metal chain that consisted of razor-sharp links. Heavy metallic boots with knives stowed at each calf rounded out his weaponry.

This creature didn't smile, for it seemed to understand its mission and the penalty for failure. His eyes never left the two men in front of him as he slowly slipped sideways in an arc trying to gain some advantage where he might, hopefully, have a clear shot at Clarisse.

Nathaniel broke the silence. "Constable, your appearance has changed a bit from our last encounter. We would prefer that you leave us in peace at this time."

---

1. An ancient weapon that combined an ax and spear head mounted at the end of a long wooden staff.

Joshua almost laughed out loud at his comment. This creature wouldn't leave them in peace, and above all else could not be allowed to leave this place. Saving Clarisse was paramount, but this evil spawn from hell could not be allowed to roam the corridors of time any longer. It would have to be destroyed here and now.

A broad smile now crept across the face of their adversary. Nathaniel posed no threat in his mind. This Kalatar from the past didn't concern him. He was more powerful than Nathaniel and he knew it. Joshua was the one he was wary of. He had engaged his kind in the future and knew their strength. "Release the wench!" he hissed. "Release her and I'll allow you to live!"

"No, that's not possible," countered Nathaniel. "You have run from me once this day. Now you face two who will see you destroyed before nightfall!"

Joshua held back. Part of their plan was to allow Nathaniel to interact with this demon as much as possible. Joshua would evaluate everything and look for the best opening to attack.

"Release her, I say!"

"Would we be considered warriors at all if we bowed to your demands? You make a poor negotiator. You're as slow in speech as you are in actions. You talk when you should fight! Do you fear your own demise?"

Taking the halberd in both hands, the demon raised the staff to chest level. They could see that the butt end of this staff had done as much damage to adversaries as the head with its ax and hook. As he moved to his right, Nathaniel moved as well, keeping himself between Clarisse and the creature.

At the same time, Clarisse slid further to the rear so Joshua might be a hedge of protection as well. She was speechless as this scene unfolded. She had experienced the evil that John Collins had wrought, but he was human, howbeit controlled by evil forces. This creature was not of this earth. Her eyes were wide and her body trembled with the realization that its only concern was her death.

"What type of creature are you?" Nathaniel teased. "You must have a name. I'd care to know what you're called so I may boast to my colleagues after I defeat you. What a privilege I have to destroy an enemy from the future."

The creature continued to move ever so slowly. "You talk too much, little human. The last thing you will see before death overtakes you will be my face, the face of a 'Karadji.'"

With that, this new adversary leaped to the right and, taking the halberd in both hands, swung it around in a huge arc aiming at the head of Nathaniel. He ducked in time and brought his own short blade to bear on the back of the attacker. It caused no damage as the soft glow surrounding the Karadji absorbed the blow. After this initial stroke, Nathaniel's blade burst into flames as he confronted his opponent.

Their enemy seemed to thrive as the battle was now underway. Joshua watched, but at the same time tried to position himself to enter the fray. Care would have to be taken so Clarisse was protected, but it would take two to defeat this one.

As the duo engaged each other, Nathaniel moved to position the creature into a crossfire. When the time was right, Joshua willed his weapon alive and attacked from the rear. The halberd blocked the flaming sword from the front, but while Joshua had full access to his back, his sword stopped short of direct contact with the Karadji. Again the glowing aura was there. This unknown shield not only prevented the contact, but also seemed to absorb the energy of the blow.

It appeared to Joshua that as this strange new villain absorbed the energy, he appeared to grow a bit in stature. *That's strange. I've never seen that before.* And with that thought in mind, he lowered another blow while the Karadji was still distracted. No change…the blow didn't phase it at all.

Meanwhile, Nathaniel was busy blocking the blows that rained down on him. Although these were potentially deadly, he was able to deflect the most injurious thrown his way. Seeing they couldn't deliver a killing blow, they fell back and gathered themselves together.

The Karadji stood tall and, realizing their bewilderment, offered a challenge. "What a meaningless attack! You have no power over me! You cannot defeat me! Attack if you will and I will not stay your hand! I invite your best! You'll find I'm impervious to your puny weapons!"

Nathaniel looked at Joshua. Clarisse hid behind the large boulder, afraid to watch but at the same time afraid to hide her eyes. The two champions acted in unison. With swords aflame, they rushed the enemy. Blow after fiery blow was attempted, but to no avail as the creature offered his body as a target. Each stroke was blocked by the unseen protective wall which absorbed the power from the attackers. Each time a blow struck home, that soft glow around his form brightened, and the power absorbed caused him to increase in size and strength.

Joshua pulled back first...and then Nathaniel. There, before their eyes, was their enemy, who was suddenly larger than before. He had grown to over eight feet now. He was more confident and his eyes now glistened with the prospect of more conflict.

"He absorbs the power of our attack!" said Nathaniel.

"We only provide him more strength with each blow that hits the mark!"

The rain continued, now a little harder. The barren area surrounding the lone boulder became muddy making it difficult to maintain their footing. Clarisse felt helpless. She wanted to help but didn't know what she could do. Her clothes soaked up water like a sponge making it difficult to move at all.

She could now see her two friends in full battle attire with no pretense of wearing puritanical clothing. Except for their rain-soaked hair, they appeared somewhat dry. The water ran off of their clothes like water runs off of a duck's back. With the rolling thunder it was hard to hear them, but she pressed in to hear their plan.

"How can we defeat such a foe?" queried Nathaniel. "Every blow that hits the mark only makes him stronger!"

"There has to be a weakness! There must be some flaw we might use to our advantage!"

They gathered around Clarisse while the Karadji waited to resume the conflict, much like Goliath waited and taunted the Israelites. Unlike the biblical story, it would take more than a stone and a sling to defeat this "giant."

"There must be a way! We're missing something!" yelled Joshua.

"We defeat ourselves by attacking him!" returned Nathaniel.

Clarisse sensed their bewilderment. There was no fear, but she knew they were searching for an answer. She played the action over in her mind and suddenly realized the answer they sought.

"Joshua, I can help! I believe I have seen his weakness while I've huddled here watching!"

The two men looked at each other. They knew better than to take her offer lightly. Already she had shown signs of maturity beyond her natural abilities.

"What is it?" asked Joshua.

"Quickly, while his confidence remains high. We may yet gain the upper hand!" yelled Nathaniel.

Clarisse now spoke with a certain amount of authority. She realized she was more than just a spectator watching her own demise; she would now be an active participant.

"That glowing aura surrounding this evil thing—it glows brightly when you attack but disappears when he delivers a blow. Even though he absorbs the power of your strike, he uses that same power against you. He may be vulnerable when he counter-attacks for the glow is gone altogether.

The two men looked at each other and smiled. It was the chink in the armor of their "Goliath."

Joshua gave Clarisse a quick kiss on the cheek. "Thank you, my dear! You've been observant while we were caught up in trying to be your champions!"

Nathaniel couldn't wait to re-engage the enemy. "I'll be first to test her theory! We'll see how much punishment he can dish out!" With that, he bounded out and feigned a fall near the feet of the giant.

The leviathan was quick to bring the ax head of the halberd down on Nathaniel. Only a lightning fast reflexive action prevented the removal of his head from his shoulders. The sword of the Kalatar blazed and stopped the ax inches from his neck. Lightning flashed as the two weapons met.

Joshua watched and quickly saw that Clarisse was correct. The glow surrounding the enemy definitely disappeared when he attacked. *He is vulnerable!* With that thought energizing him, Joshua jumped into the conflict.

The Karadji saw Joshua joining the fight and drew the large broadsword from its sheath. Nathaniel was able to roll to the side and regained his footing in time for him and Joshua to confront the creature two on one.

Joshua felt it best to reduce the number of weapons their enemy had at his disposal. As the monster attacked with another swing of the halberd, both Kalatar brought their flaming swords to bear at once. With a crack of thunder and a fiery explosive, the ax head was separated from its staff. *One down!*

As Nathaniel took up the frontal position and occupied the enemy, Joshua moved ever so slowly toward the rear. Each time their swords made contact, the air exploded with fireworks. The sound was deafening as the thunder rolled from these two weapons: the powerful flaming sword of Kalatar, and the electrifying broadsword from hell.

Joshua could see the glow around their enemy fade in and out as the battle continued. The timing would have to be perfect. Seeing Joshua moving to the rear, the alert opponent reached down and pulled a 12-inch blade from his boot. With a flick of the wrist, and at lightning speed, he hurled it at Joshua. With no time to react, the knife found its mark. Only his protective clothing kept the blade from piercing his heart.

It was all happening so quickly. The battle raged, and Joshua had worked his way into position to strike. Nathaniel was more than doing his part. The demonic adversary struck again and again with each blow being countered.

What happened next would be played over again and again in Joshua's mind. As the adrenalin pumped through his body, he tried to anticipate the absence of the protective aura. He tried…but he failed.

His timing was off, and the aura was in place as his sword met his foe. As power from his weapon was absorbed, the enemy's power was renewed and increased just as his next powerful swing caught Nathaniel's weapon near the hilt. The explosion was more powerful than anything Joshua had ever heard before.

When the smoke cleared, Nathaniel was gone. Only his weapon remained, lying off to the side where it had been propelled from the force of the blast. Joshua couldn't believe it. *What've I done?! I've killed him!*

With those thoughts, he hesitated; and that small hesitation was all the enemy needed. The Karadji took advantage of the situation and attacked. His own sword had disintegrated in the explosion, but his confidence was high. Without a second thought he picked up what was left of his halberd…and using it as a club, he swung at Joshua.

In Joshua's mind, things began to move in slow motion. He saw the wooden club coming at him but couldn't move fast enough. The contact was brutal. Blood flew everywhere as the club found its mark. His head snapped back, and before he knew it, he was on the ground rolling in the mud.

The Karadji was on him in a heartbeat. Again and again the blows rained down. Somewhere, far away, Joshua could hear Clarisse scream. Was that a dream…or real? Only his protective clothing prevented the body blows from being fatal. But even so, he couldn't take much more. He could only block so many blows to his head. He tried to remain conscious but felt as if he was about to black out.

For Clarisse, this nightmare was all too real. Nathaniel was gone in the blink of an eye, and Joshua lay almost still at the feet of his tormentor. She was horrified at the brutality this unholy demon dealt out. Within a minute or two, her husband would also be dead and their tormentor would turn on her. There seemed nothing she could do.

As she stared, she screamed. As she screamed, the sound of her own voice seemed to wake her up. The Karadji was standing over Joshua now and clubbed him over and over, incessantly. The aura was gone now, as the attack was relentless. *What can I do? I must do something!*

She looked around and saw Nathaniel's sword. Such a short blade would do no good. She inched over to where it was and, reaching out, touched it ever so slightly. It seemed to quiver as she took hold of it. As she concentrated on the emblem, it began to glow. She looked once more at the brutal scene in front of her, and with a righteous anger, she willed the weapon to life.

The flame shot forth, and with the now blazing iron over her head, Clarisse started moving toward the two combatants. The hellish ghoul had forgotten about her, so intent on destroying Joshua first. He never saw her coming up behind him. With no golden glow about him Clarisse rushed forward now, and without hesitation plunged the flaming sword deep into the back of the enemy.

The scream was ungodly. The sight was glorious. The enemy was writhing in pain at the feet of a mere mortal—the mortal he was sent to kill. It disappeared in an instant. Then all was quiet, except for the sound of the rain as it splashed in the surrounding puddles of water.

CHAPTER 25

❀

June 6, 1692. The morning sun slowly crawled over the horizon. As it warmed her cheeks, Clarisse opened her eyes. She found herself lying across the body of her husband. She could feel his chest rising with each breath he took. Lifting her head a bit, she looked around to see where she was. Had last night been a dream...a very bad dream?

No, it hadn't been a dream. There she was, covered in mud, lying with a bloody and bruised Joshua. The nightmare of the previous night was quickly replayed in her mind. *How could he have withstood such a beating and survive?* She reached up and touched his lips. *Wake up my love, wake up. No...sleep a while longer.*

She raised herself to look around. All was quiet. The rain-soaked terrain showed evidence of the activity from the night before. The battle had covered a wide area. The muddy ground revealed how widespread the fighting was. Only the huge footprints of their enemy remained as evidence of his existence.

Something caught her eye as it sparkled in the morning sun. It was half-buried in the mud, but she recognized it as the hilt of a sword. Nathaniel's sword. *Oh, Nathaniel! My heart grieves that you gave your life to save me!* She crawled to the sword, and with both hands grasping it firmly, she pulled it free.

Making her way back to Joshua, she raised his head and placed it in her lap. Stroking his hair, which was matted with mud and blood, she gently tried to wake him up. Reaching inside his coat, she searched for the little bottle of Salimar that had helped restore her to health.

Joshua opened his eyes a little and tried to smile. "Clarisse, although my body aches my eyes rejoice to see you alive." He tried to move but was unable.

"Lie still. You must rest a while before you try to move. We need to find out how badly you're injured. Try to sip a little of your healing liquid."

"What happened? I only remember being beaten about the head and body. Where did our enemy disappear to?"

"He is gone. He will not bother us again."

"Then, Nathaniel returned?"

"No. Our dear Nathaniel is no more as well." And with that she showed Joshua the sword pulled from the mud.

Joshua closed his eyes as tears welled up. When he opened them, he looked at Clarisse in a different light. "You?"

She only shook her head to affirm what he was thinking. Hard as it was for even her to believe, she had dispatched their enemy to the depths of hell from whence he came.

It hurt even to smile, but he managed a tiny one as he spoke. "Your first kill. Be proud, Clarisse. The enemy chose their target well. I know of no mortal who has ever taken on a demonic warrior before their indoctrination and lived to tell of it. What you did has provided us an opportunity to live and fight another day in the service of the Creator."

"I only did what was needed to protect you."

"I assure you that it won't be the last time that you'll save my life."

With much effort, they were able to move together to the boulder in the center of the field. As Joshua was able to sit, they assessed their situation.

Two enemies defeated with one more to go. When and where it would strike was anyone's guess. One thing was sure; Joshua was in no condition to ward off an attack of any kind at all. If this third evil spirit was a warrior type, an attack would be swift and sure.

As the morning passed, Joshua was able to determine that his injuries were serious but not critical. Every part of his body screamed as he tried to move around a little. A little water scavenged from low-lying spots in the area provided just enough water to clean his wounds. Clarisse saved enough to wash the mud and blood from her face and hands as well.

His open wounds stopped bleeding as Clarisse applied a healing balm taken from another hidden pocket of his trench coat. It would take more than this to complete his recovery. Time would be an important factor in his healing process. Yet time was something they weren't sure they'd have.

After tending to Joshua, Clarisse gathered some wood and built a small fire. She rummaged through the burlap sack they had brought and found some pieces of smoked ham and a few cold biscuits. *Not much, but it will do for now.* Her mind wandered a bit, thinking of how her life had changed. *I've gone from serving some of the best food in New England to "feasting" on a few scraps thrown together as we run for our lives. Not much to speak of, but nothing tastes better than the food that will sustain you in hard times.*

❦   ❦   ❦

Noontime came. The sun beat down and dried the surrounding area even more. Joshua didn't want to admit he was in worse shape than he was, but he had little strength to even shift his position.

"You have lost a great amount of blood my angel. We'll have to stay here till you are able to regain some strength. I know that I would not be able to row our tiny boat across the harbor even if I could push it back into the water."

"And where will we go, Clarisse? Salem Town would be a bad choice. People there believe now that I killed John Collins and you stand accused of witchcraft. With all the hysteria that the constable helped to promote, we can't go back there."

"Well, that leaves us few choices. Salem Town lies north and east of here. Once we leave this island, there is only wasteland to the south. The only way out from here would be west, toward Salem Village. If we stayed off the main roads, we might be able to pass through and make our way up to Boxford."

"Clarisse, will *you* have the strength for a journey to Boxford? I fear for your unborn child." He smiled slightly to soften his comments. "A woman with child should not make a habit of conducting hand-to-hand combat with the forces of Satan."

She caught his attempt at satire and threw the like back at him. "And husbands should not try to give their wives advice when they are in no shape to protect themselves from either his enemies *or* her wrath!"

With that said, she knelt beside him and, throwing her arms around his neck, they kissed. It was the healing balm that Joshua so craved. All their problems seemed to vanish, if just for a moment, as they enjoyed this tender embrace. "I feel strengthened already! Bring on our next opponent!" he laughed. It was a good thing for both of them…to laugh.

As the day progressed they took inventory of their remaining supplies. There would be enough for a couple of days, and then they would have to decide on their next move. As evening fell they drew closer to the fire. Resting on soft branches from the surrounding pine trees, they held each other while gazing into the star-lit sky.

"The stars are so bright tonight," she started. "It's still so hard to believe I may someday travel to these heavenly realms."

"You will, my dear. It's too glorious to describe."

"Then tell me more about your life, there…in the future."

"You'll find that my life will be nothing until you find me there. You'll have the amazing ability to watch me grow from a young child to manhood. You'll be able to see all the mistakes I'll make growing up. You'll see me as I falter in my faith, and you'll be the one to bring me back to a place of trust in the Lord. Clarisse, my life is nothing without you. Life isn't worth living without you. I love you. Through these hundreds of years we span, I'll love you."

Nothing more was said. They held each other in silent contemplation. They held each other as the embers of the fire faded and sleep crept over their tired bodies.

CHAPTER 26

❃

Three days passed before Joshua had regained his strength enough to attempt the harbor passage. Their provisions were exhausted, and they needed to get to the mainland once more. Joshua still had his battle rations that would sustain them until they found more supplies while on their journey.

Clarisse had found a spring on the island which provided enough water for her to clean their clothes. While the clothes dried over tree limbs, they took the opportunity to bathe as best they could.

Having their bodies liberated from the blood, mud, and sweat of battle, they felt refreshed as they donned their now clean attire.

"I feel like a new man," Joshua lied.

"We shall see how this 'new man' can handle the oars of our boat," she joked.

Their plan was to set out from the point they had landed and row around the island to the westward side. After a brief rest, they would head for land with the tide making it easier for Joshua to row.

It was almost comical to see these two heading back to where their boat was hidden. Joshua, unable to walk without support, trying to help Clarisse, who was unable to walk without his support. Had it not been for the gravity of their situation, they might also see their circumstances as a bit humorous. But they knew, and Clarisse now more than ever, that evil would be stalking them still. They would have to hurry so as not be caught in a vulnerable position.

Once Clarisse was aboard their small craft, Joshua pushed with all the strength he could muster to launch the boat from the rocky shoreline. After that was accomplished, he struggled to pull himself over the bow and into the boat. He lay exhausted in the bottom, his brow covered with sweat.

"We should have waited another day," she said.

"We must push on. I'm surprised we weren't discovered already. Something must be occupying our adversary. It's not like our enemies to relinquish their advantage once they've established it."

"Whoever has detained them…we'll pray strength for their souls. Their sacrifice may provide us the time we need."

Joshua marveled at how Clarisse now understood their situation. The war with evil would be fought on many fronts as the centuries would pass. Many would give their lives. She was beginning to see the bigger picture in the ever-present battle between good and evil. As valuable as she would become to the Creator's cause, she now valued the sacrifice of others.

As he manned the oars, they made their way out into the harbor a bit, but tried to remain as close to the shore as possible. Clarisse was again affected by the rocking of the boat, and Joshua, not having the strength needed, struggled to keep the rowboat pointed in the right direction. His muscles ached as he strained against the moderate waves.

Clarisse wanted to help but was paralyzed once more. She could only grasp the sides of the boat even harder as this short journey lingered longer than it should have. She could feel the bile rising in her throat, and when she could stand it no more leaned over the side and threw up.

After 45 minutes of struggling, they finally arrived at the west end of the island. After pulling into another inlet, Joshua allowed the boat to just drift to shore. He had no strength left to jump out and pull it up onto the shoreline. Clarisse held her head in her hands and moaned a little while Joshua just sat there trying to conjure up the power needed to beach their craft.

Finally, he was able to finish the last few feet of their short trip. He jumped out and secured the boat to a safe spot on the beach. Clarisse still looked white as a ghost as she very deliberately made her way to land. Together, they found a large flat rock to sit on where they could rest and recover just a bit. The afternoon sun had heated it to the point that the warmth it provided penetrated down to their bones. It felt good. No words were spoken for quite a while, each one trying to sort out, in their minds, how they could succeed in their condition.

Finally Joshua broke the silence. "We'll need to make some plans. We're in no condition to face another attack. No matter where we go, we'll be in danger. We must pray that this rest here will do us good."

"Is there no help from your heavenly brotherhood? Cannot the Lord Himself send angels from on high to rescue us?"

"No, we were blessed to have Nathaniel with us for a time. There will be no additional allies, and I know better than to risk leaving you to petition our leaders for help. When I left, my orders were very specific: one man, one mission."

Reaching inside his coat, he pulled out some of his emergency rations and once again the small bottle of sweet healing liquid. He gave Clarisse a few wafers and took a couple for himself. Though light and crisp, their sweet taste was welcomed as they washed them down with a drink from the seemingly bottomless bottle.

The refreshments helped to clear their minds and strengthened their bodies as they rested in the sunshine of the day. Evening was nearing, and Joshua took time to build a fire to take the chill off. Soon it would be time to set off again. Neither knew what tomorrow would bring, but they both knew it could be life or death. So now they took time to hold each other close, if only to feel the other's heart beating. Tomorrow would have troubles enough. Today, at this time and place, was all they could hope for.

※　　　※　　　※

Evening fell, and with it came the time to leave Jeggle's Island. Clarisse dreaded this final crossing, not only for the dangers that lay ahead, but because of the sickness that was sure to come upon her. *If only I carried not this child.* She felt ashamed for the thought, but along with it came the vision of John Collins standing over her that fateful night. *Lord, please forgive me. It's not the fault of this tiny one.*

Joshua felt better, but not 100 percent. He knew that his strength would be tested once more on this final harbor crossing. What should have been a simple feat had turned into quite a dilemma. Having his strength sapped by the strenuous rowing left them vulnerable to attack. Luckily (he hoped), the tide would facilitate the crossing with greater ease.

Once again, Joshua pushed off with Clarisse on board. This time, however, she took a few sips of Salimar before climbing into the boat with the hope that it would stem the tide of nausea from overtaking her. Hopefully this would help. The darkness enveloped the boat, and if it were only human eyes that watched they would cross undetected. They knew that human eyes were the least of their worries.

The rowing was easier this time as the tide pushed them ever closer to the shore. Even with this help, and the wind coming up from the south, Joshua tired easily. There was no conversation as they prayed for a safe crossing. Clarisse weathered this trip much better, although she was still very apprehensive just waiting for the nausea to assault her.

Joshua rowed through Ingal's Cove, and as they silently slipped by, they were close enough to town that they could hear the sound of hoofs making their way along one of the many backstreets of Salem Town. The oars were stowed for a time as they drifted along with the tide. They didn't want to draw more attention to their situation than was needed. Joshua took this brief lull to catch his breath.

When the sound of the horse and carriage faded, he once again lowered the oars into the water and directed the bow toward their goal. As they passed through Ingal's Cove, the South River gently flowed into this harbor area. A turn to the south again and they followed this to their final destination of Mill Pond.

They drifted silently under the bridge at Washington Street, and with their goal now in sight, he picked up the oars and rowed with renewed vigor. They could see the lights of the town fading to the northeast, and they knew they were approaching the Common Pasture Lands. Once there, they could disembark and make their way along the outskirts of the more populated areas.

The bottom of the boat finally came to rest in the muck of Mill Pond. It was hard for Joshua to pull it close to shore as the muck seemed to command a firm hold on his legs. The harder he pulled, the more the muck resisted his efforts. Finally he struggled until they were close enough for Clarisse to climb out of the boat and onto dry ground. They both fell backwards onto the mossy area and quickly gave thanks for their safe crossing. Silently, Clarisse gave thanks for solid ground once more.

Night was now well upon them since the trip had taken longer than expected. After hiding the boat in some bulrushes, they made their way along the edge of the pastures. Finding a small area protected with high growth, they decided to spend the night there before continuing on. A few wafers and a sip of Salimar brought renewed hope to their minds. With a gentle breeze coming from the south and a lonely owl calling in the distance they huddled together for warmth and fell asleep in each others' arms.

CHAPTER 27

❈

June 10th was the day that Bridget Bishop was scheduled to be executed. She was accused on April 4th of practicing witchcraft and afflicting pain and suffering on no less than eight people. Her accusers were prominent citizens of Salem Village, along with the Reverend Samuel Parris.

Her first public examination was conducted on Tuesday, April 19th. Ezekiel Cheever, an official of Salem Village, was in charge. At this time, she declared no less than 10 times that: "I am innocent of being a witch. I know nothing of the matter. I have never hurt a person in my life."

At the conclusion of this examination, she was told face-to-face that she had lied and would be held until an indictment was handed down. She was taken to Salem Town to await her court date in June.

In the end, on June 2nd, the Court of Oyer and Terminer, authorized by the new Governor of Massachusetts, Sir William Phips, opened in Salem Town to "hear and determine" the cases against the accused. New Deputy Governor William Stoughton presided as chief judge. The court tries Bridget Bishop, convicts her of witchcraft, and sentences her to death.

🍁 🍁 🍁

The morning arrived with birds calling out to one another and the sun hiding behind a gray layer of clouds. Summer was still less than two weeks away, so it wasn't unusual for the sun to hide a bit longer behind some lingering winter clouds.

Clarisse and Joshua seemed to awaken at the same time. Sitting up, they smiled at each other and both took the opportunity to stretch a little. Though they were both stiff and sore, they seemed to be no worse for the wear from the harbor crossing.

They were outside Salem Town and off the beaten track, so there seemed to be no rush on their part to hurry on their way. The plan was to make their way to Salem Village and go from there. If there was no indication of trouble they would move on.

There was still an outside chance that only two demonic spirits had traveled back in time to kill Clarisse. That would definitely be great news to learn. However, rarely was any intelligence information wrong. Joshua hoped this might be one of those uncommon instances.

If his work here was truly completed, he would escort Clarisse to her new home in heaven and celebrate the awesome sight of her being inducted into The Order.

Their rations were running low, so they chose to abstain from eating anything, but a tiny sip of Salimar gave them the boost they needed to be on their way.

Across open pastures and through a couple of overgrown orchards they went. They had about a seven mile walk to Salem Village, but there was a fresh water pond a couple of miles away near the Town Bridge. This would bring them closer to the outskirts of town but still off the beaten track.

As they neared the area of Blackford's Pond, Joshua grew a bit uneasy. It was the same feeling he had felt on his journey into town in March.

"There is something about this area I don't like," he started. "I have a troubling feeling Clarisse."

"This whole area surrounding yonder pond has been designated as a place of dealing with those accused of witchcraft," she responded. "If you look to the south of the pond, there is a hill where paupers are buried. I've heard in the past few weeks that they plan to build a gallows at the top of that hill to deal with those found guilty of witchcraft. I think it was only talk to scare some townsfolk."

"I hope you're correct, but I do know from *my* history that many were convicted and hanged. That may well be the place of those executions. Even so, there is a heavy presence of evil around this area."

They chose to cut across between the pond and the newly-named Gallows Hill. From the area around the pond they could see across to the bridge going to Salem Town. There on the bridge was a large crowd of people coming from town and heading toward the hill to their south. Most appeared to be following a carriage, driven by the sheriff, with one female passenger on board.

Joshua and Clarisse could see where they were going and decided to approach the hill from the backside and find out what was going on. As they climbed the hill, out of sight of those arriving on the other side, they passed through the pitiful graves of the unfortunate souls who had died with no family or money. Most were marked only with a wooden plaque that wouldn't last long in the long New England winters. Some had no markers and only showed slight indentations where someone was buried.

As they climbed to the ridge, they remained low to the ground and peeked to see what was happening below them. What they saw made their hearts stop. A gallows was under construction. It was rough, to be sure, but there was no doubt as to its future use. The long processional wound its way up the hill to this place of destiny.

It seemed a long ordeal to get the lone prisoner out of the carriage. She didn't resist, but everyone could see that no one was sure of what to do next. The officials of Salem Town were hesitant—if only because there was some part of their inner being that found this whole scene revolting. It was evident that this was history in the making and a dark page would surely be written this day.

Clarisse whispered to her companion, "Joshua, can't you stop this?"

"You know that I can't. What has been will forever be. I can't change one's appointed time of death, even for this poor soul."

"I can't bear to be a witness to this." But she couldn't stand to take her eyes from the scene either.

Since the gallows was still under construction, there was no official spot of execution. A rope was thrown over a large overhanging limb of a tall oak tree and a bench brought to the spot and placed under the limb.

Bridget Bishop was taken to the spot with her hands tied behind her back. As she hung her head, the sheriff removed a large scroll from his coat and stood on the bench so all might hear his voice.

"I, George Corwin, Sheriff of the County of Essex, now pronounce to you the sentence upon this poor soul, Bridget Bishop!

"Whereas Bridget Bishop, wife of Edward Bishop of Salem in the County of Essex, at a special court of Oyer and Terminer, on the second day of June before New Deputy Governor William Stoughton, was indicted and arraigned for the practice of witchcraft! To these charges she pleaded 'not guilty'!

"After hearing the testimony of those whom she afflicted greatly, she was found guilty of the felonies of witchcraft whereof she stood indicted, and the sentence of death accordingly passed!

"It is, therefore, in the name of King and Queen William and Mary of England, that on this tenth day of June in the year 1692 a sentence of death be imposed upon her!

"Therefore, this execution yet remains to be done!"

Bridget Bishop was then led to the bench as her feet where tied together and a dark burlap sack was placed over her head. She was lifted onto the bench, and a rope was placed around her neck.

"Say you anything before you are sent back to the one with whom you signed your name on his black pages?"

There was silence all around the scene. About 40 or 50 witnesses were there. With one long deep breath, as if savoring the very sweetness of it, she paused, and then said for all to hear, "I am innocent of these charges! I know nothing of them!"

There were those assembled there who fully expected her to repent of her "deeds" and admit to the charge of witchcraft. They were shocked, and a collective gasp was heard, when the legs of the bench were shattered by two ax-wielding men as the whole thing collapsed from under her.

Her body jerked as a fish on the end of a line and then was still. The initial shock of the crowd turned when they saw the deed completed, and an unholy roar went up in celebration that this "witch" would harm no one else. In their confused minds, the church had won a great victory.

After a time, the sheriff examined the body and once more addressed the crowd. "According to the written precept, I have taken the body of Bridget Bishop of Salem Town and conveyed it to this place of execution and caused her to be hanged by the neck until her death! At this time, she will be removed and buried in this place as required by law!"

Only Clarisse Corsairée, looking on in horror, wept for Bridget Bishop, the first person to be put to death on the charge of witchcraft.

CHAPTER 28

❧

Joshua had to force Clarisse from their vantage point to one where they'd be less conspicuous. She was reluctant to leave, as if her presence there would bring Bridget back to life. The death of John Collins she could understand, but this scene made no sense at all. Here was a married woman—who had never hurt a soul in her life—and an angry mob cried out for her death.

"Oh, Joshua…how could they?"

Joshua wiped her tears as he spoke, "The truth of this matter is that a few accusations have grown into a public hysteria. This murder frenzy is only beginning, and I fear that our enemy chose this period well. We'll need to be more careful as he'll stir this pot until it boils."

Unseen by these two, as they retreated down the eastern slope of the hill, the body of Bridget Bishop was returned to the back of the carriage and would be moved to the burial plot that had been prepared for her. Her grave would be the first in a section for witches on Gallows Hill.

Joshua and Clarisse skirted the base of the hill to avoid detection. Although it was a longer way around, they headed back into the more remote sections of the pasture lands. They knew that heading to Salem Village was necessary. They also knew that danger would lurk there.

Joshua chose not to let his wife know his deepest feelings. There would be a confrontation there. He could feel it. It would be one that would settle this matter once and for all. The presence of evil was more pronounced the farther inland they went. *It won't be long and this matter will be settled.*

Clarisse was silent as they made their way through the pastures and back out onto Country Highway. The closer they came to Salem Village the less likely they were to be recognized. It was also a fact that the closer they came to the village the more ominous the feeling was in the air. Evil had had months to work there and was deeply entrenched in the everyday life of the community.

Joshua pondered their next move. He didn't know if there was even a third enemy to worry about. He sensed that there was. His intuition hadn't failed him in the past, but why hadn't they been attacked while he was in a weakened state on Jeggle's Island? It wasn't good battle strategy to allow your enemy to regain his strength. You would normally strike while he was at a disadvantage.

The trip took longer than usual because of Clarisse's condition. Short distances covered, and then short rests, were the order of the afternoon. They found a little field corn along the way. It wasn't quite mature, but some of the early corn helped to satisfy their hunger. A few wild berries were a tasty treat as well. Top that all off with a bit of Salimar, and their strength was maintained as they traveled. In fact, the walking helped Joshua, and he felt as if he was returning to his former self once more.

They finally came to the spot where Joshua had arrived in this time period. He stood at the same spot and shared with Clarisse his feelings of being brought back 400 years and his anticipation of seeing her again.

"You say I'm near death in your future. Do you feel that our victories thus far have helped your Corsair regain some of her health back?"

"That's hard to say. I don't really know. I can't *feel* anything that is taking place in my future. It may be she'll…*you'll* only be restored to health when this war is played out, when victory is complete."

"It is strange to hear you talk of me in the future. It's as if you know two very different people."

"No…the longer I'm with you, I realize more than ever how much of Clarisse is in Corsair. I long to see her again, but I also wish to remain here, in this time, with you. I'd give up all of my future if I could but live with you, at peace, in this time."

They turned and together crossed Ipswich Road and headed on toward Salem Village on Main Street. This would lead to the center of the village…and the next stage of their journey.

🍁   🍁   🍁

The gray clouds of morning had given way to a few specks of blue sky, and the sun tried to brighten what little bit remained of the afternoon. As they walked along the way, a few carriages could be seen returning from the execution. The cheers they had heard at Gallows Hill were not reflected in the faces of those they saw returning. The solemn puritanical looks abounded on the faces of those they could see. There was no conversation that they could hear.

Main Street carried them onto Old Meeting House Road and through the center of town. They passed the village meeting house and the village church. Hoping to find a place to rest from their journey, they traveled a short distance to the edge of the village and found a boarding house with available rooms.

The owner was a Putman, Jacob Putman to be correct. They asked if he was any relation to Silas Putman, the owner of the Holystone Inn.

"No…no relation at all," he started. "There are many Putman's in New England, and especially in this area. But I am not related to *that* man in Salem Town."

It was apparent to Joshua that his friend Silas was held in low regard by this Putman. After inquiring of the owner if they might stay a while, they paid for a few days and retreated to the small room in the back of this old farmhouse. There was just a bed and a chair in the room. It was sparse to say the least.

"What are we to do now, Joshua?" Clarisse asked. "We have no possessions and no means of supporting ourselves. Surely we can't stay here very long."

"True, but the Lord will provide for us, I'm sure. Since today is Friday, it might do us well to find out as much as we can about the situation here and plan to attend church services on Sunday."

"Church! Joshua, have you so quickly forgotten what happened to us the last time we entered the doors of the Church? I'm not ready for a repeat of those horrific events!"

"No, there'll be no repeat. I'm sure of it. We'll still be on holy ground, and we'll be safe there. We must attend, or it will draw even more attention to us. Let's play it by ear and go from there."

"Why would I want to 'play with an ear'? Joshua, you make no sense."

He laughed at her, pulled her to him, and together they rolled back onto the small bed. For now, they felt safe. Safe in each others' arms. Safe in this sanctuary constructed of rough hewn logs and clapboards. And safe in the knowledge that, live or die, the Lord would take care of them.

❈   ❈   ❈

Evening was drawing near, and a walk around the village was in order—first to obtain something to eat and secondly to look around. Joshua still had some currency left over from his days of working at the docks, and there was also some left from John Collins' once bulging leather bag. Work wouldn't be an issue for a while, so they were free to gather what information they could.

The village was small and there wasn't much activity. Since this was a farming community, there would be little going on inside the village limits, but wherever they walked there was a sense of foreboding, as if they were being watched.

They came to the place in the center of the village where the church and meeting house were. The two buildings were facing each other on opposite sides of the road. On the lawn of the meeting house stood a monument to human suffering. A pillory had been constructed as a place of punishment for the many infractions a citizen might commit. The floor of the platform was shoulder height, and in the center of this raised area stood a set of stocks. Anyone who might violate one of the many local laws would find himself placed there for public ridicule.

Clarisse seemed to feel an ever-present shadow that crept along behind them, and she continually looked over her shoulder as if she might see someone, anyone, who might be watching them.

"Joshua, I'm uneasy in this place."

"I am as well. These are dark times and this is a dark place. It may be difficult to locate and identify our adversary."

"I've never experienced such an oppressive sensation. It's as if a dark blanket has been thrown over this entire area. Why must we stay here? Let's flee where we might be safe."

"I wish we could, my love, but this scene must be played out to the end. Wherever we might run the enemy has already been. They'll lie in wait for us ready to spring. We could run for months and just wear ourselves out. Better for us to stand here and fight on our terms making them reveal themselves."

As they talked they came upon an open air market where some fresh fruits and vegetables were sold by local farmers. The end of the week brought some of the best values to the villager's tables. These booths were set up and attended by some of the farmer's wives and children while the men worked late tending to the flocks and fields.

They bought a few early apples and some wild berries picked by the children. There was also some freshly baked bread available. As they walked, they nibbled on the bread and fruit, taking an occasional sip of Salimar. The bottomless flask continued to refresh and helped to encourage them a little.

"Joshua, how is it that your tiny heavenly bottle never seems to be completely consumed?"

Joshua chuckled as he looked at the small container. "Don't you recall the Old Testament story of God's prophet Elijah who ran from the evil King Ahab? A widow in the village of Zarephath took him in to care for his needs. Her concern was that she had only enough to feed herself and her son one more meal. As she obeyed the prophet and fed him first, her container of cooking oil and corn meal lasted until the prophet moved on. The Lord provides for us in the same way."

He laughed as he held the bottle to her lips for a sip. What he didn't see were the eyes that beheld this scene. Villagers saw two people laughing and being very familiar in public, with a tiny flask in their hands as well. That was more than enough to raise eyebrows as people considered the state of their condition.

They finished their walk, and, taking the rest of their newly purchased provisions, they climbed the steps to the rear door that lead to their small rented room. Their day had started early in a common pasture. It was ending now on a borrowed mattress stuffed with straw. They closed their eyes hoping for a sound, peaceful night.

Joshua slept well, but watchfully. Clarisse tossed and turned. Her dreams were filled with a replay of the events of the day. Once more they were on the ridge above the site of Bridget Bishop's execution. She could see the scene unfold again as the burlap covered her head and she heard the sound of the bench crashing into splinters from the force of the axes. Her mind could see the female form jerking on the end of the rope.

As the men lifted her down to the ground, a few of them gathered around to see that justice had been served. In her dream, Clarisse was right there amongst the crowd looking down at the lifeless body. When the burlap sack was removed from the body's head, Clarisse woke up screaming as she saw that the face of the dead woman was her own.

CHAPTER 29

❀

Clarisse woke up in Joshua's arms. He had gathered her unto himself trying to calm her nightmarish fits. He finally succeeded, and she did get some much needed rest.

Their mood seemed more somber as they prepared to head out for the day. The owner of the farmhouse prepared some coffee and gave them a few hardboiled eggs as they left and headed back toward the village.

As they approached the area where the church was located, they saw a man stepping from the church and closing the two large wooden doors behind him. He seemed to time his exit perfectly so as to meet these two newcomers as they passed his way. They assumed that this was the pastor of the church.

Reverend Samuel Parris was a man of about 35 years of age. He was the fourth man to serve Salem Village as pastor. The others before him had fallen victim to the constant infighting among the congregation.

He had spent much of his life as a merchant and "heard" God's call on his life only after a number of failed business ventures. There were critics in the church who complained that he was concerned more with his own personal finances than with the souls of the lost. He appeared to be a proud man who demanded the respect of his position.

He stepped from the doors and greeted them. "Good morning, strangers. My name is Reverend Samuel Parris. I don't believe I've ever seen you before in our village."

Joshua felt at once uneasy with this "chance" encounter. It was quite eerie. There was definitely a sense of apprehension in the air. For all their planning, Joshua hadn't even thought of whether they would try to disguise who they really were. He was caught by surprise and quickly answered, "Good morning, Reverend. My name is Joshua Lunt, and this is my wife Clarisse. We're passing through and wanted to rest a while, since my wife is with child."

"Lunt…I know not the name; however, your wife's name has a French sound to it. Would she be of French descent?"

"Would that be a problem if her deceased parents were from a French colony?" Joshua was becoming a bit irritated.

"I suppose none of us have the ability to choose our parents, but these are troubling times in our area. Some in our community would be concerned about someone who would appear different."

Joshua felt the adversarial tone of his voice and responded in kind. "Was Bridget Bishop one of those people who appeared different from the rest of your community?"

Clarisse grabbed his arm in an effort to diffuse the situation. "Now Joshua, we've no right to meddle in these local affairs."

The Reverend straightened as if rising to the challenge. "Bridget Bishop was a convicted witch! She chose to join herself with Satan, and she received her just reward! I think it would be wise for you to listen to your wife's advice! You would do well to concentrate on God's grace in these troubling times and talk little of those in league with hell's angels!"

"Of course, that would be the wish of all who cherish the written Word of God…to concentrate on His grace, not His vengeance."

Joshua could feel the hostility in this pastor's voice. "God will not be mocked! I sense a rebellious tone in your voice young man! God will use His servants here to mete out justice if that is His desire!"

Joshua knew he'd pushed as far as he should. "Of course, Reverend, you're right. Let us all hope that what is happening around us today is truly 'His desire.' With that said, I bid you a good day."

He took Clarisse in hand and strolled on down the dirt road. When they were out of earshot Clarisse couldn't contain herself any longer.

"Joshua! What are you thinking! Do we not have enough trouble without you angering the one person here that can do us great harm? For all we know, he could be our enemy here in Salem Village!"

"No, he is not possessed by our enemy, but you are correct, he could do us great harm. I feel the enemy all around us but not in a tangible way. It's as if the very atmosphere is permeated with its presence. I pushed the issue so that our enemy would be forced to show himself."

"I'm afraid that will happen very soon. I don't like this place, and I don't care to follow Bridget Bishop to the top of Gallows Hill."

※ ※ ※

The rest of the day was uneventful. No matter how hard they tried, there was no trace of enemy activity. What they did find was a village full of people who were afraid to enter into any conversation dealing with the recent trials or those accused of witchcraft.

They also continued to discover an unholy atmosphere that surrounded the entire village. Although Salem Town had its share of shady characters, this area seemed saturated with an ungodly disposition. As much as they could tell, the people seemed like honest, God-fearing folk, but they appeared tainted or stained with the spirit of fear and mistrust.

"I don't understand how an entire community could be so infected with such an awful spirit," Clarisse observed.

"This is like nothing I've ever experienced," Joshua returned. "It's hard to think that this is the work of the one last fiend from my future. We may have a hard time forcing this one to action. It seems to be part of their plan to remain cloaked in secrecy and allow those whom he influences do his evil desires."

They finished their day with a meager meal and retired early. The next day would be Sunday, and they both felt it would be in their best interests to get all the rest they could. It proved to be a good decision, as Clarisse quickly fell asleep in her husband's arms and slept soundly all night.

CHAPTER 30

❧

Since the execution of Bridget Bishop was fresh in everyone's minds, the church was full to capacity for Sunday service. No one would want to be found absent after a death sentence was carried out just two days earlier. Anyone not in attendance might be looked upon as sympathetic to those who were accused.

Joshua and Clarisse took their respective places in the designated pews of the small Salem Village church. Once again men sat on one side of the sanctuary and the women occupied the other side. The congregation was quiet, and no one looked around to see who was in attendance.

The Reverend Parris entered the room from a back door and seemed to approach the pulpit with a sense of purpose. His message would be relevant to the events of the past few days, and all who attended knew he would be at his fiery best, since he had always made clear his position on rooting out all those who might dabble in the black arts.

He dropped his large black Bible on the lectern, and the sound it made echoed throughout the sanctuary. He paused and then opened it to the Scripture he chose to use for his sermon. After what seemed like an eternity, he fixed his eyes on the congregation and spoke.

"The Lord has called me to preach. When I first received this noble calling, little did I know that there would be a great conflict that would entangle this village. Satan has desired this place, and I'll give him no quarter. We have started a process to root out those who side with the evil one, and I address those today who are in league with him.

"My sermon this day is entitled, 'Christ knows how many devils are in His church and who they are.'"

Joshua felt uneasy already. He knew this wouldn't be a "feel good" type of sermon. He looked across the room and Clarisse glanced his way in return. She tried to smile but looked anxious. He could tell this was fearful for her. Here she was, in the hotbed of demonic activity, and forced now to sit and listen to the leader of this church share his opinion with the parishioners about "devils in the church."

Reverend Parris shifted gears and spoke with authority as he proceeded with his message. "The Word of God, the only Oracle of truth, has pointed out that the enemy of mankind has been given a name by our Savior, 'the Prince of this world,' and has proven that he is a murderer from the very beginning. Peter compares him to a 'roaring lion' that rangeth abroad in the world seeking whom he may devour.

"The power of this Prince of darkness is mighty above all known sensible creatures, and his knowledge and experience manifests itself by works of wonders against both sexes. He uses divination, enchantments, and at times delusions. He is hurtful and can raise a tempest at will while transporting himself with speed from place to place.

"His minions admire him and fear him while exercising great faith in his powers. They applaud his signs and wonders and have grown to love this abomination.

"Touching the manner of his practices, he knows that the world has taken notice of him to be a liar, but continues to compel people to believe that there is no falsehood in his customs…that his ways, although counterfeit and imitations, are right and just."

Joshua looked around the room. No one seemed to move an inch. All eyes were focused on the speaker. The people here seemed mesmerized by the words he spoke.

"However…God has made a covenant with His church, binding Himself by a promise to be their God, but also requiring of them as well. The condition He requires of us is our faith and obedience.

"Satan requires a promise of his followers as well. These indentured servants of his solemnly take an oath, whether openly or in secret, to obey his rules and accomplish his desires."

There was a pause here, and everyone took notice that it was planned on the speaker's part. He looked around the room, and as his eyes roamed here and there, people looked away lest his gaze burn a path to their very heart and soul. No one wanted to be linked with those who were in league with the enemies of God.

He paused even longer until his eyes fixed on Clarisse. She hung her head and Joshua could see her cheeks blush. After a moment he could feel the gaze of the pastor on him. He looked toward the pulpit and met him eye for eye, not flinching as the Reverend Parris seemed to snarl just a bit. The Reverend broke this visual contact and once more concentrated on Clarisse.

Now she seemed more agitated, and it appeared hard for her to sit still. She shifted back and forth trying to get comfortable which only made her look guiltier (if one were looking for a guilty party in the congregation). Her face was now white, and her skin appeared clammy as the previous blush to her cheeks had vanished.

Although Joshua couldn't feel any demonic presence, he knew that this had to be part of the enemy's plan. They were trapped here and had to sit and listen to a contrived case against them unfold.

A slight smile now came across Reverend Parris' face as he continued, "Now, please, consider with me the necessary things for the people of God to know. Satan and his followers use subtle devices. We must learn of these and avoid them. But remember that they are created creatures as we are and as such are inferior to the power of our Savior.

"Even so, their power is great. We have witnesses that these followers of the evil one have the ability to change shape. They appear as angels of light at times and can change form as best suits their wishes.

"Holy Scripture tells us that this Prince of the air caused fire to consume the family of Job. Nature is at his command to devastate those who might live a holy life. It is best to point out that there are some devils and witches present at all assemblies and meetings, and therefore they are acquainted with our consultations and know the drift and purpose of men's minds.

"You must also know that this devil will also put wicked thoughts and councils in men's minds. And after a season, he labors with them by suggestions. God then gives them leave, and he will never stop his persuading until he has brought his evil enterprise to pass."

Clarisse seemed visibly shaken now. Joshua wanted to go to her but knew that was not permitted. He silently prayed for her that the Lord would give her strength.

The pastor continued, "With that introduction, I now turn to the passage the Lord would have me share with you this day."

Something was unquestionably wrong with Clarisse. She seemed as if she could contain herself no more. She rocked back and forth in her seat to the distraction of those around her. Joshua wanted to go to her but hesitated. What would be the outcome if he were to do that?

"The Scripture will be taken from St. John, chapter 6, verse 70."

Joshua could see the speaker's focus was now on Clarisse.

"This verse talks about Judas, the Lord's betrayer. Satan would have great influence on Judas as Scripture will later state. But here, Jesus makes a bold statement!"

The pastor's voice was rising now, and Clarisse felt as if all eyes were on her. She thought she would lose her mind if she stayed much longer.

"Allow me to read this verse and let it speak to this congregation: 'Have not I chosen you 12, and one of you is a DEVIL?'" And with that he pointed to Clarisse as the crowd gave a collective gasp.

Clarisse could stand it no longer. She rose from her seat and pushing people aside rushed from the building. She burst through the doors and slammed them shut with such force there were those who would later claim she never touched them at all, but rather a spell was cast as she left which slammed the doors.

Joshua was up in a heartbeat and quickly followed her while the Reverend could be heard shouting, "The Lord has spoken! The Scriptures have pointed out one here this day that cannot stand to be in this holy place!"

Outside, Joshua ran after his wife. She was about 30 feet ahead of him and was running toward the road. Before he could catch up to her, she suddenly collapsed onto the ground. He hovered over her and, taking her into his arms, held her close. She was unconscious but breathing. He stroked her hair away from her eyes, kissed her forehead, and whispered, "Dear Clarisse, don't leave me now. We're close to the finish, I can sense it. I need you to hang on a short while longer."

CHAPTER 31

❁

The church was empty now. Those in attendance were outside looking on at this dramatic scene. Reverend Parris stood on the top step of the church looking down at the fallen woman.

A man rushed forward to Joshua as if he wanted to help him. "My name is Dr. William Griggens, the village doctor. Please allow me to help. If we're able to carry her, my home is just a short distance away. We should hurry so I might examine her."

Joshua felt fortunate for the help, but at the same time a little guarded. All of his senses signaled trouble all around, but nothing specific. This doctor came from the church, which was on holy ground, so Joshua was sure he wasn't possessed. However, he had to be careful of everyone.

"Of course, thank you for the help. I fear the confined spaces of the church were too much for her. She has a fear of small places," he lied.

"Then my home would be soothing for her. I have large windows overlooking a garden which will help her to feel better. Perhaps we can escape the excitement of this morning and clear our heads while she rests."

"I would appreciate that. We've come a long way, and she is with child now these past 14 weeks. I fear this is more than she needs right now."

"With child? Why didn't you say so! We need to get her away from here quickly! She needs to lie down and regain her strength!"

And with that, Joshua picked her up and the two men left the church property and walked the short distance to the home of Dr. Griggens. Joshua looked over his shoulder as they left and could see the people pointing fingers and milling around the pastor. *I think these folks have found their next victim. Church is probably over for today.*

Once inside the doctor's home, they took Clarisse to a bedroom and Joshua watched as the doctor examined her. He felt uneasy with the doctor, but no more than with everyone else in this village. Clarisse was given a light sedative, and with a bit of water and a cool rag to the forehead, they left her to get a little rest.

The two men retired to a bigger room where they could talk and discuss her condition. "I believe she'll be feeling better soon," the doctor started. "You may have been correct that the confined space of that old church caused her to panic and leave abruptly."

Joshua still felt uneasy, but again contributed it to the overall oppression that engulfed this entire region. The doctor seemed concerned, and he remembered how helpful Dr. Browne of Salem Town had been to them. "I'm sure that the passionate message delivered by Reverend Parris contributed to the atmosphere in the room."

A servant appeared and provided some coffee for the two men as they moved to the parlor. Joshua could sense that Clarisse was resting, and he hoped to gain some insight from the doctor.

"Our good Reverend is overzealous at times, I fear. What…with all the accusations lately, it was probably his natural instinct to focus on you and your wife since you are new here."

"I think that he may be focused, but in the wrong direction," replied Joshua.

"And why would you think such a thing? It's truly a fact that many in our area have been afflicted by several of those accused of witchcraft."

Joshua took a minute and drained the cup of coffee provided for him. "There's no doubt that the devil has fertile ground here to plant his seeds of rebellion, but I fear that innocent people have been accused and that Bridget Bishop may be the first of many blameless people to meet an untimely death."

"It's interesting that you bring that up. I have just received a letter this past week from my sister in nearby Boston that addresses the same subject."

He reached into his inner pocket and pulled out a letter, folded quite neatly, and opened it as if to read. He took a moment and looked at Joshua with a slight smile.

Joshua was a little puzzled and then he suddenly felt unsteady. The doctor acted as if nothing were wrong and started, "I'll not read the whole letter, but the last part will be of interest to you.

> As I told thee in my last letter dear William, we were to meet with our friends on the night of the full moon. When we were all together in our secret place in the woods, we took time and called upon the powers of the elements to consecrate and purify our sacred circle. We then asked the help of the Goddess to provide us an escape from the persecutions that have plagued so many in the Massachusetts Bay. William, our prayers have been answered."

Joshua suddenly couldn't move. He slumped in the chair and he felt his throat closing. It was difficult to breathe and his heart was racing.

"My dear Mr. Lunt, are you feeling ill? I believe I can diagnose your problem from where I sit. You see, you have ingested a lethal dose of poison. You'll remain alive just long enough for me to finish my dear sister's letter. Let me continue.

> I hear that there have been many surprising twists in the recent course of events in Salem Village and Salem Town. The greatest irony of all must be that while these Puritans are busy accusing each other of casting spells and attending demonic Sabbaths, a coven of genuine witches sprang up undetected among them. In waging their holy war against witchcraft, those poor fools are beginning to execute innocent people. I hear that Bridget Bishop is under a sentence of death, and by the time you receive this letter, the deed may well have been done. So now the magistrates begin to congratulate each other on the progress of ridding Salem of its witches, unaware that we who truly practice the craft remain safe from their detection. What fools they truly are.
> Thy loving sister;
> Elizabeth

Joshua's mind was racing. How could he have fallen into such a trap? Poison…the one thing he was most susceptible to. He felt himself slipping away as the doctor continued.

"These fools here are looking for you to provide their next 'witch.' Your wife will do nicely. You'll be buried next to her on Gallows Hill."

As the poison took effect, Joshua's vision became more blurred, and his body felt like a lead weight. Was this the way it would end? Was he doomed to fail in his mission? As he lost his power of mental control, he could sense that his "puritanical" clothing was disappearing and the doctor would be able to see him in his heavenly garb.

"What is this? So you have the power to change your shape just as the good pastor spoke of in his sermon! What a perfect find I've stumbled upon! This congregation will have no trouble believing you and your wife are the witches they seek this day!"

For a time, his heart raced out of control, and then it slowed down. His breathing became shallow and all but stopped. *Is this what death is like?* He couldn't move at all and was at the mercy of this assassin.

Meanwhile, Griggens called for his servant and charged him to go to the church and summon the pastor and leaders of the congregation. "He'll be happy to see the fruits of his message!"

Although in a death-like trance, Joshua remained alert mentally. *Why am I still conscious? The poison should have taken effect by now and killed me.*

It seemed like an eternity before the door opened and Reverend Parris and others were ushered into the room where Joshua now lay. There was a collective gasp as those assembled there saw the state of Joshua and how his appearance had changed since church that morning.

"You see, Reverend, this one here changed his appearance just as you shared with us this morning. It was just the good Lord that directed me to his true nature and prompted me to fool him into a lethal cup of coffee. His unholy mate is in the other room and has no idea we've uncovered their disguises."

Reverend Parris stooped down to examine the body. "Are you sure he's dead?"

"Reverend...I am a doctor. I examined him while I waited for you, and as you can see he breathes no more."

Breathes no more? What is he talking about? Of course I'm breathing. How could I witness this scene if I weren't alive?

"What strange clothing! We should search him to see what he carries. Doctor, I believe that duty should fall on you."

"Of course, pastor. I thought it best to wait for you." And with that, he leaned over and opened the front of Joshua's trench coat. "My Lord, there's a sword here. What havoc he could raise with this!"

Joshua could feel nothing as the hands searched his clothing. *If only I could move. I would show them what that sword could be used for.*

"Pastor, here is a bottle, but it has no cork as a stopper. How strange it looks."

My Salimar! That's it! That's the reason I've not passed. Since I've had more than normal in my recovery, it must still be in my system working to counteract the poison.

Reverend Parris touched Griggens on the shoulder. "It would be best that the people not see such a strange sight as this. We will wrap him in blankets and bury him on Gallows Hill. It will suffice that the people understand that we've captured two witches this day. Put all his belongings with him and carry him out to the wagon that waits."

Men quickly came in and rolled Joshua over and into a large horse blanket. It took three men to lift him and start through the house. Joshua couldn't feel anything but continued to be aware of his surroundings.

Just as he was carried out of the house, he could hear the doctor say, "Reverend Parris, the other creature is in yonder bedroom. Since she is not under a sentence of death, we should notify the authorities in Salem Town."

"Yes, correct. However, it is up to our discretion to examine each person accused of witchcraft and give them the opportunity to confess. It would save a great deal of time if we, in fact, had someone who confessed. There would be no need then to notify the authorities until that was completed."

The doctor smiled and concurred that they could handle this matter best if the authorities were delayed in arriving. "I believe confession is good for the soul. I think a trip to Blackford's Pond would do the soul of Mrs. Lunt well."

The men who carried Joshua out now returned to find Clarisse waking from the sedative the doctor had given her. She could sense that something was wrong and tried to resist, but she was no match for the strong arms that forced her on her way. After tying her hands behind her back, they lifted her up and threw her into the back of the wagon where she landed next to the body of Joshua. When she saw what appeared to be his lifeless body, she screamed once and then fainted.

CHAPTER 32

Blackford's Pond was outside Salem Town just to the east of Gallows Hill. Joshua had passed it on his first journey there. He had sensed something foreboding then, and now he realized that the final battle could be played out there. *If only I could move. If only I could communicate with Clarisse.*

The wagon hurried along. The organizers of this "witch hunt" were anxious to get on with this so that there might be no interference. The wagon carrying the two accused made the trip in record time. It was followed by men on horseback, and, as word spread quickly, people rushed to the pond to see what would happen.

The wagon pulled up, and Clarisse was roughly pulled from the back. As she was thrown to the ground, she could see the wagon pull off and head up Gallows Hill to the area where Bridget Bishop's fresh grave was. The body of Joshua bounced out of control as the wagon made its way over rocks and through ruts.

Clarisse had no idea what was in store for her, but she soon saw Dr. Griggens pull up on horseback with seven or eight men behind. Others followed, and before long there was a significant number of people gathered who were quick to throw insults her way.

"Look at the witch!"

"Take her up the hill and hang her!"

"Spare her not…death to those who oppose God!"

Reverend Parris held his hand up and silenced the crowd. "People of Salem Village! Even though this wench stands accused by those in our church, she has the right to stand before you and confess her misdeeds! Allow us to talk with her before we use the stool!"

Clarisse watched as they made their way to where she was held. The doctor smiled, and the pastor looked stern. Her mind was racing with the possibilities. Joshua was dead, and she might soon follow him. *What about the future? How can God save me now? Is all lost? There must still be a way.*

The pastor of the village church started their interrogation. "Clarisse Lunt, you stand accused of witchcraft this day! Will you admit your sins and confess before God and man?"

"I will not! I am no witch! It is you who have murdered my husband! It is you who should confess this day!"

The doctor pulled close to her and softly said, "Your husband is being prepared for burial as we speak. If we cared to, we could show the people his strange clothing and how his appearance has changed. It would prove beyond a doubt you are not who you say you are."

In a voice loud and defiant she answered, "I repeat! I am no witch! God will be my judge and my rescuer!"

"Then it's time to persuade her to declare her sins! Prepare the stool!"

※　　　※　　　※

The "stool" that was called for was, in fact, more correctly named a "ducking stool." It was a device used in the punishment of slanderers, brawlers, railers, and other malcontents, as well as women who might have a scolding tongue. It was considered to be the lowest form of punishment brought over from England. The pillory and stocks were commonly used to humiliate offenders, and even the whipping post was used against more hardened criminals…but the ducking stool was the most humiliating form of punishment offered.

It consisted of a platform resting on four wheels. Two posts were positioned opposite each other, and there was an axle fixed between them. Attached to the axle was a long plank of about 15 feet in length which could be tilted up or down as the operators wished. On one end of this plank sat an armchair to which the offender's arms and legs would be tied.

Once the offender was secured, the platform would be rolled to the waters edge and the person in the seat would be lowered into the water and held underwater for differing periods of time. The usual sentence, for mild offenses, consisted of three duckings of 30 seconds in length. A long rope was attached to the other end of the platform, and when time had expired on the ducking, men would pull the platform out of the water and the process would begin again.

❦ ❦ ❦

From Joshua's vantage point, he could look down on the proceedings at the pond. He still had no movement but could hear the clanging of shovels behind him as men dug his grave. All the stories he had read as a child of people being buried alive came to mind. He quickly erased those thoughts as counterproductive and concentrated on what he could still do to save Clarisse.

He could see the angry mob around his wife and the ringleaders. He could hear her shout in rebellion tones of her innocence and the commotion that followed. *If only I could move...just a finger.* But nothing did move. He was trapped and couldn't lift even a finger to help her.

Down below, the drama was playing out with Clarisse now forcibly moved to the ducking stool. She struggled but was no match for those who forced her into the stool and tied her wrists and ankles to the chair.

The crowd grew anxious as they anticipated the procedure they had seen a number of times. Usually one time ducked under water would quickly change the mind of the most rebellious of souls.

Once she was secured, the men backed away and allowed the taunt ropes to slacken, and the platform rolled into the water to the depth that most of the platform was submerged.

"Clarisse Lunt! You now have the opportunity to renounce your wicked ways and allow the Savior to cleanse your soul! How do you respond?"

"I will depend on the Lord God to save me this day! I am no witch! Do with me as you wish!"

"So be it! Commence the 'examination'!"

Two men were holding the end of the plank, and on that order they released their hold on it and Clarisse disappeared from view as she was submerged into the murky waters of Blackford's Pond.

CHAPTER 33

Joshua wanted to scream, but couldn't. He wanted to move, but couldn't. He could hear the men behind him finishing a shallow grave and talking about what was going on in the pond below. *Please Lord, I need to help her.*

As he saw his wife lowered into the water he cried out mentally to her. He felt that she might in some way sense that he was still alive. As she disappeared from view, he felt something. *What was that? Am I crazy?* He felt he could sense her, there beneath the water.

And then, just ever so slightly, he felt a tingle. It started in his toes and was working its way up his legs. *Feeling, I'm starting to feel my legs.* But it wasn't fast enough for him. He cried out again for Clarisse in his mind. *I'm here! I'm here with you! I'm still alive!*

Clarisse couldn't believe what was happening to her. The blue sky overhead disappeared and was replaced by the dark waters of the pond. She had taken as deep a breath as she could and hoped she could hold on. The weight of the water pressed in upon her and its pressure tortured her body. She struggled against the ropes but to no avail.

For some unknown reason she felt at peace. If she was to die this way, then she would see Joshua once more, in heaven. If she confessed to the charges, she would be executed. She was at peace but would not give in to their demands.

Just when she felt she couldn't hold out any longer, she felt her body rising up through the water. As she neared the surface she heard, in her mind, an evil laugh. It was low at first then it echoed loudly as she broke the surface of the pond.

The two men controlling the plank forced her end up and out of the water. She exhaled with a great force and coughed as she tried to take in the much needed air. Her body hung limp in the chair as she gasped for breath.

The crowd cheered to see her in distress. They knew the effects a couple of duckings would have on a person's resolve. Two more dips and she would be confessing to anything.

Reverend Parris once more approached. "Has Blackford's Pond loosened your tongue any? Do you now confess?"

She still had the strength to look him in the eye and respond, "I will repeat as I spoke before! I am not who you accuse me of being!"

"So be it!" And once more the signal was given to the two men, and the chair sank again into the water.

🍁   🍁   🍁

The tingling Joshua was experiencing increased to a painful level. All parts of his body were now being reconnected to his brain. The electrical charges pulsed as his body slowly came alive once more. *Will I be in time to save her?* Try as he might, he still couldn't move.

The two men had finished their duty of digging his grave. They moved to the rear of the wagon and lifted the "lifeless" body out and, between the two of them, were able to carry him to the open grave.

I can feel them! I can feel their hands upon me!

With one big heave, they tossed Joshua into the open pit. He landed with a thud, and the men could swear they heard a slight groan come from the corpse.

🍁   🍁   🍁

Once more, the waters enveloped Clarisse. She was barely submerged when she felt an evil presence with her there in the water. Suddenly, she felt a stab of pain in her mind, and a hideous voice spoke to her.

So, you refuse to give in to these puny mortals...you'll die here then, and my mission will be completed.

She surprised herself as she calmly responded to the creature in thought. *Who are you?*

I'm your destroyer. I've traveled a long way to see that you die before your appointed time.

You're the third spirit from Joshua's future?

Yes, although you don't need that information. You only need to breathe in these muddy waters to make my strenuous trip a success.

Joshua gave his life to save me! I won't give in to you!

Then you'll die at the hands of these buffoons at the pond's edge, or they'll hang you. Either way will be satisfactory for me.

She tried to keep a clear head and made an effort to engage the demon. *What type of spirit are you? The others sent with you took form and battled openly. You hide beneath the waters of this obscure pond?*

You don't realize who you 'speak' to. I'm an ancient spirit who's incited many a riot, and legions have lost their lives without my raising a sword in battle.

The very mob that crucified your Christ was driven into frenzy by my kind. My work here, in this time, was to encourage these citizens to do my biding, and that was to kill you.

The ancient Pharisees were blinded to the truth and adhered to false teachings. The methods we used then are working just as well in this time period.

Clarisse, mentally, could feel hands closing around her throat. The water was cold, and she could feel these bony fingers dig deep into her neck. She had lost track of time, but her lungs were ready to explode. She was losing her concentration just as she was being lifted from the waters once more. The icy fingers slipped away as she broke free of the water once more.

She coughed and retched while trying to catch her breath. As she continued to gag, she lost control and vomit spewed forth as her body shook in convulsions.

The order was given, and the men manning the ropes pulled the waterlogged platform out of the water and onto the bank. Clarisse slumped in the chair, exhausted from the physical ordeal of the ducking.

It appeared that the Reverend wanted her to gain some strength before her next examination. "It would be better for her to be clear in mind and thought so she can correctly answer the questions addressed to her."

🍁   🍁   🍁

Joshua lay in the bottom of the pit thankful that he was able to feel the rough treatment he received at the hands of these "gravediggers." *Lord, just a few more minutes. That's all I need. Help her to hold on a while longer.*

He no sooner finished his mental prayer than he felt something hitting his body. The blanket covered his face so he couldn't see, but whatever it was hit him again and again. First it hit his legs, then his waist, and then his upper torso.

Dirt! They're burying me! This can't be happening! With all of his will power brought to bear, he concentrated on moving his arms. *Just a little, so they can see.* And with that thought he could feel his arms obey his thoughts. He lifted his arm and pulled the blanket back. With that task achieved, he looked up and glared at the two men who were ready to deliver two more shovels full of dirt onto him.

🍁   🍁   🍁

Clarisse was regaining her composure and a little strength. As she lifted her head she could hear the roar of the growing crowd as they acknowledged her agony. Her throat burned and her body ached from the restraints that held her bound.

The doctor made a half-hearted effort to check her breathing and pulse. The Reverend Parris shook his head as he approached her again. "Do you think you can withstand another ducking? I tell you a truth, this third time you'll not surface. There are so many things that can go wrong when lifting one from the water. Say but one word and this all stops, right here and right now."

Clarisse could hardly lift her head but her spirit was more alive than every before. "No man such as you can take my life! If I must die, it will be protecting the likes of you from unseen forces you know nothing about!"

The village pastor became red in the face and issued one last statement to the crowd. "The woman here still refuses to admit her guilt! She will receive her last ducking! May God rescue her from the evil one this day!"

She couldn't believe her ears. This man who wanted her to admit a lie was offering a prayer that might just help her. *Lord, please answer his prayer. Give me strength now, I pray.* As she finished, she could feel the wheels turn and the platform begin to move toward the water once more. A huge roar came from the crowd.

※   ※   ※

The two men were thunderstruck. They were frozen in place as Joshua slowly sat up in the grave. He brushed the dirt from his face and tried to get up. His muscles were weak and slow to respond. Luckily for him, the men above remained in shock.

As he finally stood, one of the men regained his senses and swung at Joshua's head with his shovel. Although he was weak and unsteady, Joshua was more than a match for him. He grabbed the shovel in mid-air and pulled the man toward him and into the hole. With one short punch the man was out cold.

The other man tried to yell but nothing escaped his lips. He backed away from the hole one step at a time. It was difficult to climb up, but with great effort Joshua made it. The second man continued to step back and suddenly tripped over a rock that they had removed from the hole.

Once on the ground, he covered his face so he might not see this one who was dead attack him as well. Joshua was at least strong enough to crawl to where he lay. With one simple pinch to the base of his neck, the man slipped into unconsciousness.

It was difficult and a little painful for him, but he was finally able to stand and look down from the hill to the scene below. What he saw both amazed and outraged him. The crowd below was cheering madly as the ducking stool made its way toward the water once more. He could see Clarisse, bound hand and foot, drenched to the bone from previous duckings.

He cried out to her, but the distance was too great for her to hear over the crowd. He knew he had to get to her, but he was still weak, and the terrain was rugged to the bottom of the hill. *What can I do? I must get to her!*

In his desperation, he struggled to climb aboard the wagon that had delivered him to his gravesite. He placed one hand on the seat and one hand on the wagon wheel, and with a mighty pull he lifted himself up to where he had to struggle even more to the seat. Sweat began to pour from his body as it rebelled against the effort. He looked down just in time to see Clarisse start to enter the water. *Clarisse! I'm here! I'm alive! Don't give up, I'm coming!*

❦   ❦   ❦

Clarisse saw the murky waters approaching once more. She started to inhale and exhale, practicing for that final huge breath she would take before dipping under the water again. Then…she "heard" it. Inside her mind, she heard…Joshua. *Clarisse! I'm here! I'm alive! Don't give up, I'm coming!*

She quickly looked around and saw a wagon starting down the hill from the freshly dug graves. She couldn't make out for sure who was driving, but she knew in her heart and mind that it was Joshua. *He's still alive.* It was the last thing she saw as she entered the waters again.

The evil laugh assaulted her mind again as she entered this dark domain.

So, you have come back to me. I fear that the good Reverend has no intention of you returning to the surface alive. I believe I need to accommodate him in his pursuit of justice.

Once more she could "feel" the spirit probing and touching her mind in an effort to hasten her death. Knowing now that her husband was alive, she realized that victory here was a possibility.

With a great mental effort, she "reached out" and countered with her own probing of the spirit. She could sense it recoil and withdraw.

You think you are a match for me? You have no power here. Time is on my side. All I need to do is wait. You can't hold out much longer.

Clarisse realized he was right. Even though her breath was running out she took the initiative to assault her tormentor. She reached out, once more and attacked. She found a soft spot and penetrated with a damaging blow. Once again she felt it withdraw. By this spirit's own words, it was no warrior. She felt confident, but time was indeed running out.

You dare to attack me? My demise means little. My work here is complete. The angry mob will finish you off. There's no reason for me to remain. But I'll leave you something to remember our altercation this day.

Clarisse then felt a stabbing blow to her mid-section. Her body screamed in pain and her mind focused on the child within her. *No! Not that!* The pain was so excruciating, she exhaled all the air in her lungs and her body slowly went limp.

🍁 🍁 🍁

Joshua hurried as best he could down the hill. It was difficult to manage the team of horses because he still struggled to control his body. The crowd below was chanting, but he couldn't hear what they were saying.

The men who were manning the ropes that pulled the platform from the water had been relieved of duty. He could see them walk away shaking their heads. It was quite obvious that the intent was to leave his wife in the water, killing her.

Because of his inexperience with horses and his struggle to regain use of his body, the wagon and team made quite a commotion coming down the hill. People suddenly took notice of his descent, and a few pointed in his direction.

As he got closer, he could hear what the crowd was chanting. They weren't chanting at all, but rather were counting the seconds and minutes Clarisse had been under water. The usual 30-second time limit had passed, and the mob was counting at 30 seconds times three. *How can she still be alive?! Lord, please give her grace now!*

Now he was close enough to be seen by the doctor and pastor. Their eyes were wide as they saw him pull the team into the area of the "examination." He drove past them and pulled up to the edge of the pond where the ropes connected to the platform were tied.

As he jumped from the wagon, he felt some strength returning to his limbs. With a running start, he dove, head first, into the murky waters and disappeared from sight. The crowd roared even louder because they had never seen anything like this before.

As he made his way along the length of the plank, he drew his sword. He was ready for anything but hoped he would only need it to cut the ropes that held Clarisse. He found her limp body in the chair and hurriedly cut her free. He pushed off from the platform and brought her to the surface. Once there, he lifted her into his arms and carried her out of the water.

The crowd was certainly worked into a frenzy at this sight. Joshua, in strange clothing, was rescuing an accused witch, snatching her from the very jaws of death. They weren't sure whether to run away or attack him. The Reverend and the doctor moved to intercept Joshua as he made his way to the wagon.

From under his coat he pulled his sword, and raising it high above his head, it instantly burst into flames for all to see. Most people fell on their faces or fled. Reverend Parris answered this by raising his Bible in the air. The doctor pulled a gun from his pocket and pointed it at Joshua.

He laid Clarisse in the wagon then turned. A shot rang out, and the crowd that remained became silent. The lead ball had struck Joshua in the chest and fell harmlessly to the ground. He smiled and bent over and picked it up. Tossing it at the feet of the shooter he said, "You meant all this for evil, but you don't know the victory that has been won here this day."

He jumped onto the wagon and quickly drove off. He was learning fast how to control the team, and when they reached the main road, he turned them to the east and headed for Salem Town. He could see men mounting horses to pursue them but he felt he had a safe lead…enough of a lead that he stopped to attend to his wife.

Her breathing had stopped, so he hurried to perform mouth-to-mouth resuscitation. After a couple of minutes, she coughed and water poured from her mouth. She was weak, but breathing now. He turned to drive the horses once more, but she stopped him. "Oh Joshua, the baby!"

He looked and could see the damage done. She had miscarried. "Clarisse, I'm sorry." He held her and cried with her. Even though conceived in horror, the child was part of her.

"They'll pay for this!"

"No, it wasn't these humans, but the third creature we looked for. He waited for me in the pond."

"Then he's gone?"

"Forever, my love. I'm so tired though."

Suddenly they heard a shot. Joshua looked back and saw that the mob was in pursuit. He jumped to the seat and slapped the horses with the reins spurring them onto the town. He tried to stretch the distance between them but could not. After all they had been through, the last thing he wanted was for her to die at their hands.

He hurried up Essex Street and through the town. He turned this way and that way, traveling the back streets he learned about in months past. Finally he came to Becket Avenue and turned toward the desolate area where Clarisse's cabin was. Up the deserted path he went and pulled around to the rear of the house.

He jumped down from the seat and rushed to the back of the wagon. Clarisse tried to sit up but was weak. Joshua knew their time was short and they would need to hurry to make their final run.

"Clarisse, I know you're faint, but the time has come for us to go home. I'm worried about your strength, but I feel we've accomplished our task here. Do you think you can make it?"

"We've been through so much, my love; a trip to your heavenly home would be but a small risk at this time."

"It's not my home any longer, but *our* home."

They could hear the sound of the mob approaching. They were still vulnerable, and Joshua knew it. After all, the third demonic spirit told Clarisse that the mob was incited to do his bidding. They needed to hurry. As he concentrated on the small clearing, the light began to shimmer.

The first of those who chased them rounded the bend and pulled up short as they saw the huge shimmering waterfall and the deafening roar it produced. With all they had seen and heard already, the sight before them was too much for some to handle. A large majority turned and disappeared down the narrow path. A few fell to the ground and could be heard praying to God. Others remained frozen in place and couldn't take their eyes off of the scene before them.

What they saw was beyond their belief. Joshua, with Clarisse Corsairée in his arms took one leap and disappeared into the multi-colored cascading waterfall…this part of his mission completed.

CHAPTER 34

Joshua had made this trip numerous times through the years. Except for his first passage, each trip was a thrill unmatched by anything on earth. He knew, however, that Clarisse would be bewildered, scared, and wondering if she would survive this supernatural transition from her natural realm to the heavenly kingdom.

Unlike Joshua's first journey, at least she knew her intended destination. When he had first stepped through the heavenly portal, he didn't have the assurance of his immediate future like Clarisse did. In fact, he expected instantaneous death for attempting to gain access to a place where he wasn't permitted. He felt at the time that he could do no less than to try to save Corsair.

As a 21st century Kalatar, Corsair's mission was to gain the confidence of Joshua and orchestrate his entrance to their heavenly compound. As her mission played out, he thought that she was being called back as punishment for their involvement with each other. They had fallen in love, and there was a question of possible consequences for their actions.

In reality, part of his testing was to see if he would risk all to give his life for another. He passed the test, but that very first passage was difficult on his physical body. He wondered now how Clarisse would manage given her weakened condition. Her first journey would take a few detours before her final destination was reached.

🍁   🍁   🍁

For Clarisse, the sound was more than deafening. In her simple 17th century existence, there was nothing that could possibly compare to the noise assaulting her ears. As she entered the vortex, it seemed her body was being stretched and pulled in every direction. She couldn't catch her breath, and she felt as if her very spirit was being sucked from her body.

Her eyes couldn't adjust to the rapid fire, ever-changing kaleidoscope of colors, and the strobe-like effect made her nauseous even though she held her eyes closed tight.

She couldn't feel anything solid beneath her feet, but she sensed movement and a rushing sensation as one might feel in a boat rushing toward a waterfall. Faster and faster she seemed to move along. Her body was now spinning as it moved, and she wondered if she was actually dying. *Oh, Joshua! Are you here with me? I need you!*

After what seemed an eternity (although it was in fact only minutes), she felt a slowing of the movement. She couldn't see or hear anything, but her nausea subsided as she discerned a shift in movement. *Definitely slowing.*

As a caterpillar spins a cocoon around itself and awaits the time it emerges as a beautiful butterfly, so now Clarisse could feel herself being turned over and over as a soft silk-like substance enveloped her body. She couldn't move a finger. She couldn't talk, although she tried several times. She heard nothing now as she was covered from head to foot in this heavenly casing.

With just an instant to catch her breath, she was unprepared for the next leg of her journey. In the blink of an eye, she felt herself being shot upward as if she were a tiny pebble in a celestial slingshot.

She didn't know how long this part of her trip took, but she marveled (in her mind) what a remarkable turn her life had taken. If all that Joshua had told her was true, then her life would truly never be the same. *The former Clarisse Corsairée may very well be gone! If I survive this, what wonders I shall see! All for God's glory!*

She just finished that thought when she sensed her movement had stopped as well. She could feel a solid platform beneath her but could not move any part of her body. She was held fast in her heavenly shell. There was no sound, and the thick covering over her eyes prevented her from seeing any of her surroundings.

Little by little, the heavenly strands that held her fast melted away, and she could now feel a little more freedom. Although her sight was blurred, she saw movement all around. Figures moved here and there—some of whom seemed to be attending to her while others passed by on either side.

Her hearing may have returned, but those around her made no sounds as they effortlessly moved her onto a strange table. Once aboard, she seemed to float along as they made their way up one shiny metallic hallway and down another.

She couldn't see Joshua but felt that he was nearby. The sensation was similar to what she felt on earth when he was near, but it was now more intense. It was as if this "sixth sense" was dominant while her other senses were at a diminished level.

A soft glow of light seemed to seep from the walls as she was quickly moved through this unknown complex. She still couldn't speak or move, but she felt a peace that she never knew before. *Safe...I finally feel safe. Oh, where is Joshua?*

❦   ❦   ❦

Joshua had finished his transport no worse for wear...as usual. He saw Clarisse was being attended to and trusted that he would be there when she was conscious. He remembered his first passage and how, when he finally realized he hadn't been killed in the crossing, he had turned to see Corsair, beautiful as ever, standing close behind him.

For now though, he had things to attend to. A delegation had met him as soon as he arrived, and even though he wanted to stay with Clarisse, he knew he couldn't.

Lucius was there to meet him, as well as others of The Order. *How strange...Lucius doesn't know me yet.*

"Joshua, we are honored to have you with us," he started. "Congratulations on a victory that will echo through the very corridors of time!"

Others chimed in, and a hardy chorus of cheers went up. There were no Kalatar there that Joshua recognized even though he knew that some of his comrades in the future pre-dated this time period.

Joshua felt it time to address this group. "Thank you for your welcome and your help. Although my journey's been long and this effort a difficult one, I couldn't have succeeded without the help of a fallen comrade. Nathaniel gave his life for the success of this mission, and I sorely mourn his loss. The day will come when we can all praise our Lord as risen saints with him before God's throne."

Suddenly the crowd parted, and one lonely figure responded to Joshua's remarks. "I fear, dear friend, that the reports of my death are a bit premature!"

"Nathaniel! How?! What?!" Joshua was speechless. He rushed forward and grabbed his friend to make sure that what he saw before him was indeed real. As he did, he noticed that Nathaniel was nursing some serious injuries.

"I'm still a wee bit under the weather," he winced.

When Joshua regained his composure he asked, "How did you survive the blast? I saw you completely incinerated!"

"Don't always believe your eyes. I was able to escape the mortal realm just as our friend the constable directed his full fury on me. Although badly injured and out of the game, I was able to finally make my way back, and I've been on the mend ever since. How is your dear wife, if I might ask?"

"She is here among us…among friends. I must get to her before she awakens though."

Lucius approached Joshua and motioned for him to follow. Joshua removed himself from the group and stepped aside to listen to what his future unit leader had to say.

"Joshua. This is in truth a moment never before seen in all of heaven or earth. A human surviving the journey back to this time period let alone orchestrating the defeat of hell's chosen ones. It's quite a privilege, even for an immortal spiritual being like myself."

"Lucius...the honor is mine. It's a great opportunity to meet you. You'll serve as my unit commander in the distant future. In that era, I'll go where you direct me to go, with Corsair by my side. But now, if you have nothing more for me, I must get to Clarisse."

❋   ❋   ❋

Joshua made his way through the winding corridors until he came to a room similar to the room he had left Corsair in. As he looked through the doorway, he saw Clarisse laying in a bed and being attended to by a host of beings.

He remembered the last time he saw her in this condition...and the way she reacted to his presence. He slowly entered the room and cautiously made his way to her side. *No reaction. That's good.* Feeling confident, he closed the distance between them and settled in by her side.

"How is she doing?" he asked.

One of the beings smiled and commented, "Remarkable! Although she was bruised, battered, and exhausted from her encounter with those who meant to kill her, she has 'crossed over' in very good shape."

"And what of her *other* injury?"

"Alas, the child within is no more. There was nothing we could do. The loss occurred while she was under water. It's amazing she survived at all. She's a very strong mortal."

"Yes...very strong."

Then Joshua noticed her eyes flutter just a bit. He reached down and held her hand and whispered her name. "Clarisse, I'm here."

She opened her eyes, and it seemed as if all of the tribulations of the past few months melted away. She smiled and tried to speak, but couldn't.

"Don't try, not just yet. It'll be a while before you recover and adapt to your new surroundings. It's finished, Clarisse. We've won. You've shown by your victory why it was so important we rescue you. No other mortal could have taken on hell's own as you did. This is a great day. Stories will be told of your courage and valor for centuries. Satan chose well whom he needed to destroy, but he failed."

With no way to verbally communicate with her husband, Clarisse pulled him close and tenderly kissed him. As their lips parted, their eyes met…and once more this connection proved to be all that was needed. They became lost in this silent world. It would become a world all their own, like nothing in heaven or earth.

CHAPTER 35

In the weeks to follow, Clarisse slowly recovered from her injuries. They were weeks of constant visits from Joshua, Nathaniel, and others who were excited and curious to meet this newcomer to their ranks. It was beginning to sink in how special she was and how she had already gained great respect from even some of the most seasoned veterans.

After she recovered, there were times of indoctrination, and training was started as soon as she was able. There were times she still felt like the insignificant waitress from the Holystone Inn, but she was quick to learn and take on her new responsibilities as well.

Joshua was able to be there for her first glimpse of this new heavenly expanse she found herself in. Walking with her and showing her the wonders of the heavenly complex was special for him. After all, she would escort him around, to his wonderment, 400 years later.

It was exciting for him as she stepped out of their confines and onto a balcony for the first time, viewing the great vision heaven had to offer. Their sanctuary was a small floating city surrounded by other islands in the "sky." These islands moved as if in concert with one another. Winged creatures flew back and forth issuing forth praises of God and the Lamb that was sacrificed all for mankind.

Far below them she saw the streets of shiny gold pavement with trees on either side which bore special healing fruits. A river flowed back and forth through this great scene, and it was all too breath-taking for Clarisse. Tears rolled down her face at the amazement of it all. She clung to Joshua in awe of all this, and he held her close.

"This is just a glimpse of what our Creator has provided. We're allowed access to only a small area. I long to see all He's provided for us."

"When will that be?"

"When He chooses. We may die in His service, or we may live to see Him return with the forces of heaven at the Last Trump. Only He knows. Until then, we'll do His bidding."

"Will you be by my side until then, my dear?"

With that question Joshua turned away from her gaze.

"Joshua?"

"I've talked with Lucius today. I requested that I be able to stay in this time period with you. I shared with him what a great benefit it could be for The Order if I remained here…with you. I have knowledge that other members of The Order don't have. We would have a great advantage through the ages."

Clarisse reached out and turned his face toward her. The saddened look he now had mirrored her own expression. "You're leaving me? No! We fought the forces of hell to be together. Why must we part now?"

"It's been determined that if I stay, there could be too many instances where my actions, here in your timeline, would affect the future. There'll be no descendants of John Collins because of me."

"And there would be no Corsair in your future if you hadn't stopped that monster!"

"I know. It was a necessary action. But we couldn't minimize those actions in the near future. Lucius also indicated that even if I remained here my life would end on the day of my birth in the future. I can't exist in the same timeline with myself."

"But we'd have 400 years together."

"Yes, but we may have more than that in the future. Either way, it's been decided. I have no vote in this matter. The High Council has decreed it to be so."

Clarisse held him close and cried. Joshua could hardly stand the thought of leaving Clarisse…his wife. They had gone through so much to get to this point. The thought of leaving her was unbearable. It was like nothing he had ever gone through before.

Together, they stayed on the balcony in each others' arms as long as they could. When they could remain standing no longer, they moved inside and went to bed, holding each other until sleep overtook them.

❦   ❦   ❦

Who knows how long Joshua stayed in the 17th century? The time he spent in the spiritual realm, with Clarisse, could have been but a blink of an eye in earthly time. But in real time, he was with her for months.

She recovered, of course. But there followed weeks of intense training and instruction. She seemed be a natural at everything she attempted. There were those who felt that her early exposure to the enemy helped her. She knew first-hand how it felt to engage the army of darkness.

Different instructors mentored her in the use of various weapons she would need to know about. Although not presented yet with her own flaming sword, she became skilled in the use of this, her primary weapon.

She became stronger, physically, due to her new environment. She was faster and more alert because of her heightened senses. She was keenly aware of Joshua's near presence even more so than when they were on earth.

Clarisse shared with Joshua the feeling she had right before they met for the first time. It mirrored his experience in the future when he met Corsair.

"I remember that first night having a strange feeling I'd never known before. Something, or someone, was close. I *felt* it. It wasn't a sense of danger; I would learn that feeling later. But when I looked up and saw you, this unknown stranger, all seemed perfect.

"When I looked into your eyes that night, for just an instant, I saw strength and power, and…love. I knew we'd be together."

He held her close once more. "How strange to hear you describe those feelings, because I will experience the same thing when I'll meet you for the first time in my future."

This comment saddened her once more. "I can't bear the thought of you leaving. How can I go on without you?"

"You'll go on with the knowledge that we *will* meet again and our love then will have new meaning, *a deeper meaning*, than ever before. Our love will be one that will span centuries! No one can say that but the two of us. We will live and love, and fight, together for God's glory as He needs us to."

❦ ❦ ❦

When Clarisse's training was completed, it was ordained that she be inducted into the ranks of The Order of Kalatar. The ceremony was rich in tradition and ritual. Her induction was more meaningful than others had been because all of heaven now knew of her and how she entered into battle as an untrained mortal. Usually these ceremonies were private and closed. But it had been decided to incorporate this induction with a great victory celebration that all of heaven could enjoy and rejoice in.

The great council chamber would be used for this celebration. As Joshua entered, he was amazed that nothing was different from the council chamber he had left to come here. The same chairs were in place, the same rows of seating circled the indoor arena, and the same heavenly creatures flew back and forth praising God from the rafters.

A great host of angelic beings were present, as well as many Joshua recognized from his future. His part in this saga wasn't lost on any of these witnesses, for they knew the consequences they would have suffered had his mission failed.

The crowd in the chamber rose to their feet in reverence as he entered. He acknowledged their respectful admiration but quickly motioned for them to be seated once more. He wasn't the one to be honored here today. Clarisse would be the one to shine brightly.

With all assembled, Lucius entered, and behind him other unit leaders…followed by Clarisse. She was dressed in white from head to toe. The long dress she wore touched the ground, and it looked as if she floated instead of walked. Her long auburn hair flowed down past her shoulders and was gently tossed back and forth as she walked—as if an unseen breeze was blowing.

She was never more beautiful to Joshua than she was at this time. As if on cue, she motioned for him to join her as she made her way once around the council chamber and then stopped near the center of the room. They remained standing there, hand in hand.

All eyes were on her, and everyone rose as a sign of respect and thanksgiving. God had provided, once again, for all creatures great and small. He once more used the most willing vessel to meet the needs of mankind.

Lucius motioned for all to take their seats and signaled for the induction to begin. A podium rose from the floor with two items on it. One of the items was a jewel covered insignia that bore the symbol of Kalatar. The other item was the heavenly crafted flaming sword which would, in the future, dispatch legions of demons to the depths of hell.

Lucius lifted the insignia and held it high above his head. The heavenly gemstones caught the light and sparkled brilliantly for all to see. He then walked slowly to Clarisse and pinned it on her dress. "Clarisse Corsairée, this emblem is a symbol of all this Order holds dear. It signifies the wearer is one of great courage and honor. It shows all who look upon it that you have completed the highest levels of training and garner the respect that comes with that position. You have earned the right to wear this, and I present it to you today. May our God be blessed to have you as a warrior among our ranks!"

A cheer went up from all who were assembled there. Never before had any there heard these words uttered. It seemed appropriate that they hear them at this particular presentation.

Lucius stepped back, and Joshua stepped forward. It was tradition that one member of The Order welcome a newcomer and present him with his own awesome weapon…the Kalatar sword.

Joshua respectfully lifted the sword from the podium. He held it high as Lucius had with the insignia. He turned toward his wife and spoke: "Clarisse Corsairée…my faithful life companion. It's my honor to make this presentation today. Even before your entrance here, you wielded a weapon like this in battle. No other mortal has ever willed a weapon to life as you have. No other mortal has ever engaged the enemy and lived to tell of it. And no mortal deserves this honor more than you. I present this weapon to you and welcome you into our Order…The Order of Kalatar! May God richly bless your time in His service as you meet His enemies in the many years to come!"

Clarisse had tears in her eyes and took firm hold of her new weapon. She hugged Joshua and refused to let go. When she finally released him, she gave him a long deep kiss, something never seen before in a ceremony like this. She then turned toward the crowded assembly and, raising her sword high above her head, willed it to life. It burst into flames for all to see.

With that came cheers from all corners of the chamber. Lucius looked around in wonderment. Other Kalatar rejoiced along with the angels in attendance. It seemed as if it would go on forever, but it couldn't. Lucius held up his hands finally for all to be seated once more.

"What you have witnessed this day is unusual, to say the least. These ceremonies have been closed in the past. With this induction also comes an unprecedented event in our history. Kalatar Joshua, who has come from a time in the distant future, is required to return from whence he came. It's an event ordained by the High Council and will be witnessed by all in this chamber."

With these words, Clarisse held Joshua even closer. The tears were flowing freely from their eyes as they knew their time together here was drawing to a close.

Lucius continued, "We owe Joshua our very existence. Without his courage and skills, the enemy would have easily killed Kalatar Clarisse and our futures would have changed forever. We salute you this day, Joshua!"

With that said, all stood again and cheered wildly. Joshua hung his head and cried even harder. *What good is victory if I lose Clarisse now? No…I'll see her again, in a moment, in the twinkle of an eye, she'll be there waiting for me.*

While the crowded room continued to celebrate, a fearful sight invaded the council chambers. Joshua had seen this before. It was the frightful cascade of fiery lava he saw at the start of this extraordinary adventure. The massive room immediately fell silent. All eyes were on Joshua and Clarisse. A long embrace ensued as the two lovers and friends said their 'good-byes.' Their lingering touch finally slipped away and Joshua dove headfirst into the blistering portal of time.

Epilogue

❈

Joshua entered the black, silent world he had experienced previously. He knew now what to expect. The silence, the ringing in his ears, and the absence of light was not as suffocating as before. He could see the gateway appear as he sped, out of control, toward it.

The energized electrical-like storm appeared, and he knew that he would soon be drawn through with a peaceful calm to follow. He was ready this time, and as he entered the vortex, his body was prepared for the experience.

It happened once more in a split second, the stretching and pulling on his body. The strain was great, but this time he knew he could survive it. He knew he *would* survive to see Corsair once more.

Then it happened...as before. The images appeared in his mind's eye. Events unfolded as before except this time the events moved forward in history. Great historical events rolled out as a filmstrip on a giant reel, only he was the only patron in this "theater" attending the private showing.

He was a witness to life's greatest triumphs and tragedies. Ordinarily this all would be of great interest to him, but his only thoughts were on seeing Corsair again. *Corsair...Clarisse...how should I address her?* He felt like a schoolboy on a first date, anxious to see her again, but nervous at the same time. After all, this time he would see her in his timeline as his wife.

As the events flew by, he noticed he was approaching the time of his adulthood. He grew more interested and wanted to see these events now that Clarisse's future had been changed.

He once again stepped to the edge of the moving stream of time, and events slowed so he could watch them unfold in his life. He viewed his former self, selfish and egotistical. He laughed to himself as he saw the materialistic drive he had to succeed in business. How stupid and vain it all was. *Vanity of vanities...all is vanity.*

He witnessed his failed attempts at relationships and felt ashamed of himself in the way he treated women. They were only objects to be hunted and bedded. *How shallow.*

His heart leapt at his first glimpse of Corsair. How beautiful she was. He could see how she had arranged their incidental meetings and all of the suspicions he'd had about her were planned. He watched as she displayed supernatural abilities that puzzled him. He *felt* the electricity of their first touch.

Now he could see himself climbing the stairs to her apartment for a pre-arranged dinner date. There, behind the door, she slowly removed a silver ring from her finger and placed it in a miniature jewelry box. *She knew...all the time, she knew!*

He spent the night in her apartment, but she allowed no inappropriate behavior as he was used to. However, he knew this was a different relationship than any he had ever experienced. *Her eyes...so captivating. What secrets does she hide from me?*

Then there was the fateful morning after. She explained so much to him, but there was so much more to hear. She led him to believe her attraction to him was possibly forbidden...and then the fearful call "home" to stand and answer for *her* actions.

As he saw the waterfall of colors and the roaring thunder for the first time, he knew she had told the truth. As she entered the "portal of judgment," he dove in after her as if he could save her—when in reality it could have meant his death.

In the time stream, Joshua moved forward and saw his own induction and Corsair presenting him with the sword that now hung on his belt. *A little faster now.* He moved on and witnessed their first battles and the rescue of Linda Carson. Each event viewed a little differently now that he realized his wife was mentoring him as he had her.

He missed her. His heart ached to the point he felt it would burst, and so he dove headlong into the time stream once more. He needed to hurry on his way. He had to see his wife again.

History quickly unfolded but he had no interest anymore. Only one thing was on his mind, only one thing seemed important…to see his wife once more.

❦   ❦   ❦

It happened quickly. Faster than he thought it would. It was like slamming on the brakes in an automobile. The vehicle stops but the body wants to continue forward. The momentum Joshua had built up forced his body forward as he was spit from the mouth of the vortex. One instant he was in the netherworld of time, the next he exploded into the room he had left.

He was on the floor looking up. There were his companions standing as if they had just seen him off on his extraordinary journey.

They were as surprised to see him as he was to see them. As a matter of fact, some doubted that he left at all. Then, there was a cry from an outer room. "Hurry, come quickly! It's Corsair!"

Joshua was up and running with speed that surprised even himself. The others were left to follow behind. Down the hallways he flew, and along the way others could sense the urgency of his quest.

Finally he came to her room. *Corsair…Clarisse? Who will I find?* He was almost afraid to look into the room for fear she might still be in bed. But he did look. There before him, standing in radiant white light, was Corsair, dressed in the flowing white gown she had worn at her induction. She was even more beautiful than ever.

"Clarisse, my love."

"Joshua…I've missed you so much," she whispered.

He ran to her and cherished the warmth of her embrace. Her lips were on his once more, and when they parted, her eyes became the window to her soul that he so longed for on his journey home. As they stepped back for a moment, she reached up and unclasped a chain from around her neck…and taking a silver ring from it, she placed it on her finger…there to remain evermore.

The End

978-0-595-41450-5
0-595-41450-8